JOLT

Visit us at www.boldstrokesbooks.com

JOLT

by

Kris Bryant

2014

JOLT
© 2014 By Kris Bryant. All Rights Reserved.

ISBN 13: 978-1-62639-191-8

This Trade Paperback Original Is Published By
Bold Strokes Books, Inc.
P.O. Box 249
Valley Falls, NY 12185

First Edition: September 2014

Credits
Editors: Shelley Thrasher and Ashley Bartlett
Production Design: Stacia Seaman
Cover Design by Sheri (graphicartist2020@hotmail.com)

Acknowledgments

I would like to thank my parents for always encouraging me to put my thoughts to paper and being proud of me. I would also like to thank my sister, Patty, for always being there for me during the good times and the bad. Thanks to my incredible friends Debbie, Patty, Rachel, Jennifer, Lucy, and Boz—your support and laughter gets me through all the stress and craziness of my life. To Foxman for flaring up my creative side since we were kids, and to L. Snow for her honesty and advice. I love you all!

Thank you, Bold Strokes Books, for taking a chance on this story and for my editors, Shelley and Ashley, for getting more out of me than I thought possible.

To S.B.

Always…

CHAPTER ONE

Whenever a conversation turns ugly or someone repeats the same thing several times, I recite poetry in my head. I don't think it's rude. People need to get their story out, but I usually grasp what they're saying the first time they tell me. By the third time, Emily Dickinson and I are deep in conversation.

It's early June at Camp Jacomo in middle Missouri, and Val, a camp counselor, and I are struggling with a fence that fell down earlier in the week. Okay, she's struggling with it, and I'm standing there watching her. She's about six feet tall, with short, short hair, and looks great in a tool belt. She'll ask for help when she really needs it and gets offended if anyone tries to help before the words come out of her mouth. Not that she's allowing them to because she's been talking nonstop about an altercation one of the counselors got into with a townie last night. That's not a good thing for the camp's reputation. Our camp for children of gay and lesbian couples is one of a kind. Because of the sensitivity of our clientele, we have to be careful with the locals, as well as any visitors that come along.

"Can you believe she said that?" Val asks, wiping her dirty hands on her jeans. Ah, that's my cue. I pause with Emily and focus on Val again.

"Have you said anything to Renee?" I ask, falling right back into the conversation, as if I wasn't just in a carriage with Emily, Death driving us somewhere. I'm concerned for the safety of the camp because we simply don't need any extra attention.

"Nah, I'm sure it'll blow over soon. I don't want her to worry. You know how it is when the newbies get bored with camp life and camp rules," she says, shrugging like it's no big deal after all. She hops on the fence and hands me a water bottle. I don't need any water because I haven't exactly worked up a sweat, but I take it anyway. I, too, jump on the newly mended fence and sit next to her.

"You should probably tell Renee just to give her a heads-up in case someone surprises her with it. The new counselors don't know how important this is for the kids and their families," I say. Our conversation ceases as we hear a car driving toward us. "I wonder who that is?"

"Let's hope it's not the sheriff about last night!" Val elbows me in the ribs and knocks me off balance.

I don't know a graceful way to fall. In what feels like a awful scene from an old French movie when something bad happens in slow motion, I can see myself falling backward and don't realize it's really happening until I land with a not-so-soft thud in the prairie grass below. I'm not quite sure how long I stay on my back, but after my eyelids flutter a few times and I find my breath again, I inventory all moveable body parts to ensure they're still moveable. Ten fingers, ten toes, two legs, two arms. Yep, all still good. The sharp rocks digging in my back are probably going to leave bruises, but I don't care. I'm just happy I'm not really hurt. I'm embarrassed and briefly think of a way to retaliate.

"Oh, my God! Are you okay?" Val's suddenly by my side looking down at me.

"I'm fine," I say, laughter bubbling up. I tend to laugh at the strangest times. Since I've had the wind knocked out of me, I'm really not in a hurry to get up.

"Are you all right?" someone asks. Tilting my head backward, I see a woman leaning forward with a very concerned expression. Her long brown hair hangs over her shoulder, and, for the briefest moment, I have the urge to reach up and touch it. The smell of lavender and vanilla instantly fills my senses. Two of my favorite smells. I stare at the small flecks of gold in her caramel-brown eyes and then focus on red lips full with promise. Within five seconds, my entire body explodes with warmth, excitement, and fear. It's a welcome feeling after the anguish of the last three years, but extremely unnerving. Realizing I'm staring at her and not answering, I mentally slap myself on the forehead and sit up.

"I'm fine, thank you." I'm surprisingly quiet, examining bits of grass in my long blond hair and some dirt on my leg. How did that happen? It wasn't as if I rolled on the ground when I got there. Or did I? How could I have possibly gotten "Pig-Pen" dirty from a simple fall? "I probably shouldn't have been sitting on the fence," I say. I almost shake my head at the stupid things coming out of my mouth, but I tend to ramble when I'm nervous. Especially around beautiful women, and this woman's pretty much straight from my list of everything I've ever looked for in one. When she reaches out to help me up, I almost pass out again, this time from glee.

Before I reach out to the stranger, Val's yanking me to my feet.

"I'm so sorry. I didn't mean for you to fall." Val can't keep herself from laughing. I can't blame her. I'd do the same thing. She hugs me, then turns to introduce herself to the beautiful stranger on her right. "I'm Val and this klutz here is Bethany." She grins.

I want to slip away because I'm not only embarrassed about falling, but because Val has called me a klutz. So much for first impressions.

"I'm Ali. Ali Hart. Here to see Renee and Darren Thomas," she says with a smile. A perfect smile. One with straight, white teeth and confidence. "Am I headed in the right direction?"

She obviously hopes one of us will help her, but it'll have to be Val because I'm a mess. I'm about ready to go find Emily and check out of this conversation, but Val quickly saves me.

"The camp is just over the hill there." Val points. "We work there, too. Renee and Darren are up at the main cabin. You can't miss it."

"I can give you a ride if you want. Maybe somebody at the camp can look you over in case you bumped your head," Ali says.

When she turns to stare at me, I can actually feel my heart hammering. Now that I'm standing, I get a look at the rest of her. She's about five feet nine, roughly four inches taller than me. She's slender and has skin as pale and probably as smooth as marble. She's wearing jeans and a black short-sleeved blouse, her brown hair pulled back in a single clip. I can't take my eyes off her hair. It's so long and wavy, and again I find myself wanting to wrap my hands in it, the strong desire taking me by surprise. Ali Hart is absolute perfection.

"Thank you, no," I say. "We have a few things here to finish up before lunch." Yeah, like I'm a lot of help, but I can't be around her. Not yet. I need to collect myself first.

"Well, then I'm sure I'll see you both later." She walks back to her car.

"Holy crap, Bethy. Do you know who that is?" Val elbows me again, and I'm seriously tempted to break her arm at this point. I'm thinking, yes, a very beautiful woman who has just taken my breath away. "She's like a famous singer. I hear her music on the radio all the time. What's she doing here?" she whispers to me out of the corner of her mouth.

Ali waves a quick good-bye and puts the car in drive. As she passes us, she smiles when her eyes find mine, and something so foreign, so different, so exciting fills me. Maybe I'm reading too much into her glance, but for the first time in almost three years—maybe for the first time in my life—I feel a jolt.

CHAPTER TWO

Lunch on the weekends is usually around one, but I can't muster up the courage to head to the kitchen knowing Ali Hart is there. A part of me wants to run and absorb everything I can about her, but my inner wallflower holds me back. Who is Ali Hart? Val mentioned that she's a famous singer, and something in the back of my mind tells me I know her name. How does Renee know her? Not that I expect Renee to consult me on the camp's daily activities, but a heads-up when a beautiful woman is expected sure would be nice.

I decide on an apple and a yogurt for lunch that I scavenge from my tiny refrigerator and head out to the porch. I really need to work on my book. Book four in my murder-mystery series is due at the end of summer, and I haven't given it the love and attention it needs. I've also been working on something new that I find therapeutic, but it too requires serious time and effort. I'm not a great oral communicator, but I can write. When I'm angry, I write. When I'm lonely, I write. When I'm hurt, I write. My editor, Tom, read some of my gibberish and asked that I continue sending him chapters. So now I'm committed to two separate works. One is fiction, the other I wish was. As hard as I try, I can't stop my mind from drifting back to Ali and our first meeting. I groan with embarrassment. Why was I so tongue-tied around her? Why didn't I say something clever? I'm that girl who always thinks of the perfect thing to say several hours later, when the dust has settled and nobody is around to hear. I head back inside and fire up my laptop to Google her. I'm not proud of my blatant stalking.

After reading about her very public life and staring at photos for about ten minutes, I can feel my eyes burn. I need to sleep. I haven't slept since yesterday morning, and I'm going to need some rest before the kids show up tomorrow. Some nights I keep writing until the words stop. I don't mind though. It's my way of life. I close my laptop and slide it on the coffee table. I'm asleep in about ten seconds.

My cell phone startles me awake, and I hold it in my hand for a second until I get my bearings. "Hello?" I mumble, knowing I sound like hell, but sleep is heaven, and whoever's calling better have a very good reason for waking me up.

"Will you be joining us for dinner?" Renee asks.

"What time is it?" I'm slurring my words.

"Do you mean dinner or what time is it now?" Renee used to be a schoolteacher and is forever correcting all of us. I have a degree in English from Northwestern University and feel like I'm still in grade school around her.

"Yes." She knows what I mean and I know what she means.

"Dinner is at seven thirty. In roughly twenty-five minutes. Can we expect you? And how are you feeling? Val told us about your fall," she said.

"Did she mention that she pushed me, too?" I ask, my ten-year-old self shoving past the adult in me. I shake my head and quickly change the subject. "Who all will be there for dinner?"

"The gang. And our guest, Ali. So can we expect you?" she asks again.

A part of me wants to race around and get ready, while the other part wants to stay hidden on this couch. I know what I have to do though.

"I'll be there. Need anything?" I ask out of respect.

"Just your beautiful self. See you in a bit," she says.

I snort in response and hang up. Before total panic sets in, I mentally race to the closet and pick out something nice, but not too nice. It always takes a few seconds for my body to catch up to my mind. By the time I'm actually standing at the closet, I'm down to twenty minutes. I don't have time to wash my hair, but I do have time for a quick shower to wash the sleep and dust off. I grab a pair of white linen shorts and a light-green sleeveless blouse and head for the bathroom. I'm very much a girly girl. I wear jeans only when absolutely necessary. My wardrobe is all skirts, blouses, slacks, and heels or sandals, and I'm pretty confident that I'm the only one at camp who wears Victoria's Secret thongs. When I'm down in the dumps, a nice outfit always cheers me up.

I decide to keep my hair down instead of throwing it up in a ponytail or a bun. I have surfer-white hair, even though I don't surf, and light-green eyes, thanks to my Danish and Irish heritage. Renee's granddaughter thinks I'm a mermaid, and, when nobody's around us, I pretend that I am. She's in awe of me. I'd like to keep it that way for a few more years. I forgo any makeup because spending the last week in the sun has given me a nice glow. I know we aren't supposed to be in the sun anymore because of skin cancer, but I live in Chicago and hide in a high-rise ten months out of the year. Feeling the sun warm my skin is incredible, and I just can't give that up yet. Plus with a tan, I don't have to mess with makeup, and that's fine with me.

I head to the main cabin, eager to be around Ali again, but excited, too. From my online searching I learned that Ali is from the East Coast, comes from a large family, and has a girlfriend. The girlfriend part bums me out, but it doesn't surprise me.

"Look who decided to join us!" I hear Rob, the camp's head counselor, say as I open the screen door to Renee's kitchen. He holds his wineglass high up in the air to toast me and winks. Several other counselors cheer so I bow playfully to my audience. I see Ali and Renee off in one corner. I steal a glance at Ali and smile. She really is beautiful. She's wearing a long silky skirt that almost reaches the floor and a white short-sleeved blouse. Her hair is down like mine, but hers is several inches longer. She looks more like a mermaid than I do. I glance around to find somebody to talk to before she realizes that I'm staring.

"Sorry, I fell asleep," I explain to everybody as they gaze at me expectantly. Apparently, somebody said something to me that I didn't hear. I'm sure I've said the right thing, but Ali's presence momentarily distracted me so I'm not sure.

"We were worried that maybe you had a concussion," Rob says. "Heard you had quite the spill."

I know he's joking, but I'm still embarrassed. I can feel the color heat my cheeks and I shake my head, recalling my afternoon.

"It wasn't a big deal. Val accidentally pushed me. I'm fine, but I'm sure I owe her a bruise or two." I glare at Val. She blows me a kiss and tilts her wineglass at me. I sit next to Rob when I suddenly feel the hairs on the back of my neck stand tall. Without turning, I know that Ali is sitting directly behind me on the bar stool.

"Hello." Her voice is quiet and warm.

I turn around shyly, hoping she doesn't see the chill bumps across my bare arms. I'm amazed my physical reaction toward her. I've never been a sexual person. I never thought the explosive passionate interludes in books or movies were real. Yes, I've felt passion, but not to the point where I forget about my surroundings. This is why I'm completely thrown off by Ali. I've said what, three words to her, and I can't seem to get ahold of myself. My stomach is quivering, and when I look at her, I want to touch her. I want to know if her body is as smooth as it looks. I want to feel her curves and run my hands down her tiny waist and skim over her flaring hips. Again, I'm suddenly aware of how quiet the room is, and I know I need to say something because in less than a second, it'll become uncomfortable.

"Hi." I smile at her, and she smiles back. My smile gets bigger and I mentally scold myself. I feel like a total groupie and I don't even know her music yet.

"How are you feeling?" she asks, concern in her voice.

"More embarrassed than anything. I'm fine though. Thanks for stopping to check on me. Are you settled in?" I wasn't about to tell her about the two rather large bruises I found on my backside in the shower. I want to change the subject anyway.

"This is a really great camp," she tells everybody.

"How long are you going to be here?" Val asks.

"I have the entire week off from my tour, so as long as Renee wants me here, I'm yours."

If only she was saying that to me. I think about my online stalking again and mentally frown at my misfortune.

Renee announces that dinner is ready and it's buffet style. I hang back a bit to distance myself from Ali. It's exciting to be near her, but I need to stay away so I don't start crushing on somebody who has a girlfriend. That's the logical side of my brain. The creative side is already scoping her out. I notice her long fingers and the grace of her hands. Even though they seem delicate, they must be powerful and strong. She wears a silver ring on her thumb and another silver ring on the ring finger of her left hand. My heart sinks because that means she's not available. I call on Ms. Dickinson and Mr. Frost for support. Emily feels my pain, but Bob is no help. He's encouraging me to pursue her, knowing full well I shouldn't. I'm going to have to ditch him and hang out with Em for a bit tonight. She's more reasonable. She knows the power of mentally stalking someone while remaining completely passive and quiet. Tonight, we decide to talk about being nobodies in a sea of people. I prefer it that way and she agrees.

From what I can gather, the dinner conversation is going well. I'm able to tune out everybody except Ali. Maybe it's because I'm not familiar with her voice, or maybe it's because I want to hear it. It's lilting. That's a word I don't think I've ever used before, but it fits Ali. Even if I didn't know she's a singer, I'm sure I'd have figured it out. Sometimes when she speaks, it sounds as if she's already singing. Rob and Sandy, Val's girlfriend, are telling Ali what to expect during the week with the kids. I turn my attention back to my meal and continue my discussion with Emily. We've moved on to one of her favorite topics: God. I save those conversations for when I really need to tune out the world because she's pretty intense about Him.

"Why are you so quiet tonight, Beth?" I hear Rob say my name and am forced to press rewind and recall the entire question. I'm flustered, but I collect myself and answer.

"I'm just working out my story in my head," I lamely explain. They don't need to know the truth.

"Are you almost done?" He continues to prod me, then turns to Ali. "Bethy is a writer. She hangs out here every summer and works on her books." My cheeks heat up again. I see Ali's brow lift slightly and know he's piqued her interest. I quickly look away, not wanting this conversation to take place. I like my anonymity here at camp.

"I love to read. What do you write?" Ali asks me. There's no way around it. I'm going to have to make eye contact. We do, and there it is again. The jolt. My eyes widen at the intensity of her look, but I do my best to stay calm. I take a deep breath and answer.

"Mostly mysteries. Some poetry. Just whatever needs to get out of my head," and my heart, I add silently. I never talk about my work. I'm very protective about it. Especially my new book. I still have mixed feelings about having it published, but Tom assures me it's brilliant and really will help others. I think he just loves a good soap opera.

"Well, we're proud of Beth and will leave her alone until she finishes it, won't we, Rob?" Renee says, understanding my discomfort. The table laughs at her scolding, and he hangs his head in shame. The conversation turns back to Ali.

"Will you play us something after dinner?" Sandy asks Ali. She smiles and nods. She strikes me as the type of artist who loves to play for small groups.

"I think we have time for a few songs. Just let me run next door and grab my guitar." She jumps up from the table and waves off everybody who's objecting, promising it isn't an imposition at all and she wants to do it.

"I like her already," Renee says, sounding completely at ease with Ali.

"I'm surprised you didn't mention her to us," I say.

"Surprise! I really wasn't expecting her to answer my email. When she agreed to come here, I was so excited. Her music is great and the kids will love her."

As if on cue, Ali returns with a well-used Martin guitar and one of her killer smiles. Val and Rob move the furniture around to make room while the rest of us quickly clear the dishes away. Ali sits on a stool and strums her guitar for a bit, tuning it. I'm tense and make myself relax. I've always fantasized about a relationship with a musician. The minute Ali breaks into song, I'm enthralled. Something inside me opens up, and a rush of warmth and excitement dances in my veins. I shudder at the intensity of it. I'd chalk this up to my normal infatuation with rock stars, but this is something more. I want to look away, but I can't. I want Ali to look at me, but I don't. I've never heard Ali's music before today and honestly don't know that I can handle it. My body is tense again and an electricity surrounds me. I glance around to see if others in the room feel it too, but they're all sitting back and smiling, oblivious to the combustible force I'm fighting. Ali finally makes eye contact with me and I gasp. The heat returns and my body swells. I have to leave. I can't stay here a minute longer. As soon as she finishes her song, I jump up, do a quick wave to everybody, and bolt out the door. Every strum of her guitar follows me back to my cabin, and I can't close the door fast enough. She's fantastic. I have to stay away from her. I'm not good at this. I'm not good at relationships. I'm not good at pretending everything's fine. I'm sure as hell not good at heartache.

CHAPTER THREE

I'm surprised to see a light on in the fitness room. It's well after midnight and I'm pretty sure I'm the only one awake at camp. I peek in the window but don't see anybody. I'm hoping to find Sandy or Val in there so that I can sneak in and scare the living crap out of them. I punch in the code and push the door open. A slight movement to my right startles me, and I'm suddenly staring at an almost-naked Ali Hart. She's wearing a black sports bra and tiny low-riding yoga shorts. Her flat, hard stomach is dripping with sweat. My eyes travel up and down her body, feasting on her erect nipples straining hard against the sports bra. I envision myself touching her stomach, running my hands over her tight, slick muscles. I actually ache to touch her.

"You scared me." Ali's voice is low and almost raspy. I quickly make eye contact with her, blushing at the look she shoots me. She caught me gawking at her and I can't cover it up. Thankfully, she doesn't call me out even though we both know. I clear my throat and apologize for scaring her. I head to a treadmill, the piece of equipment farthest away from Ali. I can feel her eyes on me the entire time. I don't know if I'm excited or scared, and I'm struggling with wanting her to leave or stay here with me. I quickly stretch, then jump on the treadmill, thankful the humming noise is enough to drown out any conversation she might want to have.

I can see her in the mirror working out behind me. She's lifting weights, and I can't help but admire her lean and long body. The only meat on her is muscle. Her hair is pulled back in a ponytail, exposing her shoulder blades, and I'm practically drooling at the muscles that bunch every time she lifts the weights above her head. I'm incredibly turned on and incredibly confused. Yes, Ali is attractive, but I live in downtown Chicago where I'm surrounded by all different shapes and sizes of beautiful women. Not one has caught my attention or given me a spark until now. And this isn't just a spark; this is a raging inferno. What is it about her? I can feel tiny quakes in my belly and squeeze the treadmill bars to keep from outwardly shaking. I'm pissed at myself. I'm angry because she's unavailable and because, even though I know that, I still want her. I try everything I can to get my mind off Ali. I sing "God Bless America" twice because I can't find Emily or Robert anywhere. It's too hard not to look at her. She's twenty feet away from me. I watch her out of the corner of my eye. I never thought sweat was sexy. I always made my ex-girlfriend, Crystal, shower after she worked out because I didn't want her touching me. I can't understand this obsession with Ali and her sweaty body. Even when Ali busted me staring at her dripping wet six-pack, I still kept looking. I need to focus. I can't remember the last time I fantasized about a woman. Hell, I can't even remember the last time I masturbated. It was probably about six months ago and only to fall asleep. I know I haven't done it because I was turned on and needed release. I'm almost positive Crystal packed up my libido in one of her suitcases and took it with her when she bolted. After the initial shock of having my lover abandon me, I eventually became numb to the thought of another relationship and the thought of sex. I don't want to trust another woman with my entire body and soul and have her destroy me. Not even for a moment of passion. I've never been a promiscuous person. I've only had three lovers in my life. The thought of a one-night stand gives me the creeps. I place too much emphasis on romantic love. Probably too much, but it's worked for me in the past and made me happy. Or so I thought before seeing Ali bathed in sweat.

Ali wipes down her weights, then heads my way. I can't do anything except maintain eye contact. She turns on the treadmill next to me. I smile at her, then focus straight ahead. I fear that if I don't, I'm going to trip, fall face-first, and smack into the wall behind me.

"Why are you up so late?" Ali asks.

"I normally don't go to bed until late. I don't need a lot of sleep. What about you?" I try to sound casual.

"My concerts usually last until almost midnight. Then it takes a few hours to unwind. I had all this energy and adrenaline and no stage to burn it off, so I decided to come in here." I can think of about six different ways I can help her burn off that energy, but I keep that to myself. "Besides, exciting things happen late at night." She smiles at me and her eyes narrow. I think she's flirting. I stumble and grab onto the bars to catch myself. The last thing I need is to fall in front of her. Again. Warm, strong fingers wrap around my arm to steady me, and my knees feel weak again.

"Are you okay?"

I nod. "I have a nasty little habit of falling in front of you."

Ali laughs. I turn off the treadmill. Apparently, I can't walk and talk around her. She surprises me by turning hers off, too. Guess we're going to talk.

"Are you done already?" I ask because I don't know what else to say.

"I guess so." She grabs a towel from the rack. I watch her quickly wipe the sweat off her face, neck, and stomach. I feel awkward staring at her. I need to get out of there. I open the door for us and say a quick good night to Ali without looking back at her. I really don't want to be rude, but I just can't. I can't allow myself to feel anything for her.

❖

The next morning isn't any better than a few hours ago in the fitness room. I don't know if I'm subconsciously seeking Ali out or if fate is guiding me, but I'm constantly running into her. Literally. On my way to the kitchen, I jog up the steps to the door reading a letter from Renee that she sent to all of the counselors, and my hands smack into a pink cotton T-shirt. Someone grabs my shoulders to stop me before my head can do any damage. I know who it is before I can even make eye contact. I already know her smell. How is that possible? I want to fade away like this didn't really happen.

"I am so, so sorry," I mumble, hardly able to make eye contact. She hasn't moved her hands from my shoulders. Her touch burns. Finally, I look up and stare into her caramel eyes. She's smiling at me. It's more of a wicked grin and I'm wondering what's on her mind.

"Where are you going in such a hurry, mermaid?" she asks. I turn bright red because I know she's been talking about me with either Renee or her granddaughter or, worse, both.

"I really need to pay attention to where I'm going." I realize my knuckles are still brushing her stomach and quickly drop my hands.

"I don't mind you running into me." She releases me, but her fingers touch my face and she gently brushes away a piece of hair. I'm pretty sure she lingers on my cheek for a few seconds longer than acceptable, but this whole experience has me disoriented and time seems to have stopped. Now I'm really confused. I don't know if she's playing with me, hitting on me, or what, but yesterday I read that she has a girlfriend, a live-in-let's-buy-a-house-together type of partner. I'm disappointed and kind of pissed off because, in my mind, she's perfect and would never cheat on her partner. She'd never hit on another woman out on the road. I must look pissed because she quickly steps away from me. "Renee's inside if you're looking for her," she tells me and walks away. I watch her, my emotions swirling around, some of them identifiable and some I'm not sure I've ever had before.

Chapter Four

Can somebody run into town and pick up what we need?"
Renee asks the group. I'm just about to slink out the door
when I decide getting out of camp is a good idea. I've been
hiding from Ali all week. It's Thursday morning and I haven't
spent one minute alone with her since Tuesday morning on
the steps of the kitchen. Val and I volunteer simultaneously. I
grab the truck keys off the table when I hear Ali's sultry voice
in the other room asking Sandy if she can tag along to drop
off some mail. My palms start sweating. I tell myself she'll be
gone in forty-eight hours and I can survive a simple trip into
town with her in my personal space bubble. I'm still irritated
with her flirty attention. I want to bring up her girlfriend, but
I can't even talk around her. Plus, then she'll know that I've
been researching her and that might just encourage her more.
I round the corner and brace myself. To my surprise, Ali is
gone.

"Where's Ali?"

"She ran to get her mail. Where have you been all week?
You haven't been around much," Sandy says.

On Tuesday I talked Britney, one the newbie camp
counselors, into switching workloads with me. She gets to play
with the kids, and I get to wash clothes and clean up breakfast

and lunch dishes. It's busy work, but it kept me focused on something besides my growing obsession with Ali Hart.

"This is my behind-the-scenes week," I say. Val gives me a weird look but doesn't call me out. That was my job last week, too, but Sandy doesn't realize it.

"Okay, I'm ready." Ali returns, waving a stack of letters. "Thanks for waiting."

God, she's gorgeous. Her hair is in a French braid, pulled over one shoulder. I have no idea why her hair fascinates me so much, but I have to force myself to look away. She looks puzzled and I do my best to ignore her. She crawls in the back with Sandy, and Val slips in beside me. I'm thankful Ali isn't next to me, but I can still see her in my peripheral vision.

The grocery store is only a ten-minute drive, and we split up as soon as we get there. Ali volunteers to go with me, while Sandy and Val head to produce. Suddenly, I'm a deer in headlights. She points to the aisle and starts walking. I follow and she slows down until I catch up.

"I've really enjoyed myself this week," she says. "You haven't been around much. Have you been engrossed in your book?"

Her eyes catch mine. She has the prettiest eyes I've ever seen. They're flirty and fun, and I can tell she's a happy person. Why shouldn't she be? She's famous, beautiful, in the prime of her life, and probably has the perfect life with her girlfriend. I'm not jealous. I don't know her well enough to be jealous.

"I've been busy with it. It's hard to just stop writing." I wish I was telling the truth. This week I haven't even tried to write. "That's why I've been doing more of the necessary evils around camp, because my schedule has been messed up."

"Like working out at one a.m.?" She winks. Her smile is infectious and I find myself mirroring her grin. We're walking to meet up with Sandy and Val when I hear somebody calling me.

"Bethany! How have you been?" I turn around and see Sara Phelps approaching me. Wonderful. Sara runs the town's five-and-dime store and recently came out after a twelve-year marriage. She's a beautiful woman with dark-red hair and bright-blue eyes. She's about my height but has twice the curves I do. As much as I want to like her, I just don't. She seems high maintenance and very demanding, and I'm allergic to those two traits.

"Hi, Sara. I've been doing well. How about you? How's business?" I introduce her to Ali and explain that she's with us for the week, but Sara looks bored. I smile because I know when she runs across Ali's name in the future, she's going to kick herself for being rude.

"You should come by the store and see all the changes I've made. Besides, I need help with my website and you're good with a computer," she says. I mumble something noncommittal and say good-bye. I'm so uncomfortable. Ali is quiet as we head to the checkout lane. I don't see Val and Sandy sneak up behind me. We are all quiet until we climb back into the truck. Val waits a solid minute before opening her mouth.

"Well, she did everything she could to get your attention." Val pokes me. I'm embarrassed. I'm trying to be calm around Ali and another woman hits on me. "Maybe you should just go out with her. She's totally into you and she's got a smoking-hot body," Val says. I groan.

"Maybe you should give it a try," Sandy says.

I blatantly ignore them.

"Maybe Bethany's just not interested," Ali says. "It's uncomfortable when people push you into something you don't want to do."

I want to high-five Ali, but that seems childish, and I'm too nervous to touch her anyway so I just shrug like it's no big deal.

"All right. We won't push, but at least think about it. It's like riding a bike. Once you get back into the seat, you'll know exactly what to do," Val says.

I'm absolutely done with this conversation. I know Val and Sandy want me to move on and they're only pushing me because they love me, but their timing sucks.

"I know." I appreciate their concern, but they're revealing too much. I'm private and don't like having such a personal conversation in front of a new person. A new, exciting, and sexy person, but new to me and my past. Ali must sense my discomfort because she suddenly changes the subject and I silently thank her.

"So do the townspeople ever visit the camp?" she asks Val.

Val is very much the spokesperson for the camp and loves to hear herself talk. Bingo. I can now check out of this conversation. Great. I seek out Lord Byron and we discuss beautiful women. I'm sure that has everything to do with Ali and nothing to do with Sara.

"The smiles that win, the tints that glow," I recite to myself—one of my favorite lines ever written by him. Okay, apparently I've said it aloud because everybody is staring at me.

"What?" Val nudges my shoulder and looks at me as if I'm nuts.

Thank God we're back at camp. I choose to ignore her. I can't slip away soon enough. We unload the car, and Val and Sandy head for the kitchen.

I search for something to say to Ali. "Thanks for changing the subject earlier."

"Well, Val was pushing it and you were obviously uncomfortable," Ali says.

"I know they're only trying to help."

"Apparently, they think it's time for you to get back out there." She grins.

I give her a tight smile. "Thanks again for saving me." I grab my stuff and make a quick exit. I know I'm snubbing her. I'm also rude and not being a good host, but I'm upset. Not really at Val, but just at my situation and my inability to let things go and move on. I wonder about how many missed opportunities I've let slip through my fingers. Val's right. I need to take that chance again.

CHAPTER FIVE

I grit my teeth as Renee breaks down the afternoon for me. She wants me to work with Ali and the kids because Britney, Ali's original helper, isn't feeling well. I'm staring at Renee like she's crazy. I can't work with Ali. I can't be around her for more than twenty seconds. Boom. Just like that, I've slipped away. I can hear Renee blabbing on about something, but I'm too busy talking to Mr. Frost. His words are eloquent and vivid, and I can tune out everything and visualize his words. He's very calming.

"So, it'll only be for a few hours in the afternoon, just until we break for dinner. And maybe help with the concert tonight. Just keep the kids in line and make sure they pay attention to Ali. You know how they get if they think they can take advantage, and you know how sweet Ali is."

I want to puke right now. I have to rewind the conversation several times before I can process it. Renee is patiently waiting for my answer.

"Why can't Val do it?" I whine. I can't believe I'm a successful thirty-year-old woman. I sound like a twelve-year-old. Renee looks at me like a tantrum-throwing child, and I immediately stop my rant. Instead, I roll my eyes and head toward the gazebo where Ali is with the campers. I can already hear her guitar and I'm gritting my teeth, anxious for any reason to get me out of this predicament. I try my best to look calm and cool and stroll up the steps. Ali looks at me and smiles. Some of the kids wave to me. Sometimes I can be such an ass.

Ali's great with the kids. She's so patient, especially with the young ones. Do she and her partner have kids or does she have any nieces and nephews? Judging by how comfortable she is with them, I'm going with yeah. Right now she's showing Matthew, a ten-year-old, how to properly strum a guitar. She's asked him to help her during the concert, and within a few short hours, Matthew has gone from quiet kid to camp rock star. I'm smiling at his beautiful transformation.

Ali winks at me. It's amazing how I can be angry and happy at her at the same time. What is that? I want to be mad at her for being flirty, her girlfriend probably patiently waiting at home for her return, but I just can't. Maybe I'm reading too much into her winks and I just haven't been around nice people for the last several years. I shouldn't assume that she's flirting.

"Maybe Miss Bethany would like to sing with us."

I'm already shaking my head before I even process the entire conversation. I'm still building fences with Mr. Frost, and I'm thankful he's keeping my mind off Ali and our close proximity. Singing with her is an absolute no. All of the kids start pleading and begging, and I wave them off and shoot Ali an unpleasant look. She catches my drift because she focuses their attention back on her. She strums her guitar and nods to Matthew to join her. I cringe at my rudeness and am surprised she's still polite. The kids start singing an oldie camp song and I can't help but smile. It's an awful song and they sound dreadful, but they're all smiles and seem to be having fun.

Ali is their only saving grace; her voice is strong and

soothing. After hushing Mr. Frost, I close my eyes for a moment and focus on her voice alone. It really is nice. It's smooth and fiery like a shot of brandy. After they finish their song, I open my eyes to find Ali staring at me. The look she sends jolts me. I sit up straight and look at the kids. They're looking at me expectantly. Once again, I'm wracking my brain trying to figure out who just asked me what. I get nothing, so I apologize to everybody and wait for somebody to ask me the question again.

"How did we sound, Miss Beth?" one of the smalls asks me. We refer to any child under the age of nine as a small. I smile because they sounded horrible, but I nod and praise them as if they're all angels singing perfectly on key. Ali smiles at me knowingly and I can't help but smile back. She has enchanted these children, and I'm questioning why I'm here to help her. I'm definitely not needed.

"Do you have a song suggestion for us, Miss Bethany? It's been a while since I've been at camp, and I can't remember all the songs." Ali is smiling, but I can tell she's pulled back from me. I'm sure it's from my indifference to her.

"Well, how about something that's on the radio? Does it have to be a camp song?" That gets the kids excited. They're shouting out songs they know, and Ali's trying to calm them down. I step up and walk over to her, facing the kids and waving my hands to get their attention. "Okay, okay. Let's do one at a time. We need to make sure Miss Ali can play the song, too."

I'm standing about two feet from Ali, and her nearness is affecting me again. She looks great today. Her hair is pulled up into a messy bun, and the sleeves of her thin plaid shirt are rolled up past her elbows, showing off the corded muscles of her forearms. Her shirt is unbuttoned and she's wearing a simple, white tank top that clings to her curves in all the right places. I haven't forgotten the magnificent body under her clothes. She's wearing jeans and has to be hot, but Christ, her long legs look fantastic in tight denim, and I'm selfishly glad she's wearing them. Yeah, I could spend days just on her legs alone.

"Beth?" I look up at Ali. Shit. Did she catch me staring at her again? I want to melt away right here on stage. "The kids are thinking of a Miley Cyrus song. What do you think about that?"

"Can they learn the song by dinner?" I look at my watch. We only have about four hours to practice. We decide on an older Miley Cyrus song, God help me, because most of the kids know it. Ali runs back to the main cabin to print sheets of music while I give the kids a quick bathroom and expel-your-energy break. Her guitar is resting on her chair under the gazebo and I can't help but touch it. Does Ali have a name for it? I can see some wear and a few scratches, but it's beautiful, and I know she makes incredible music with it.

"You can pick her up if you want." Ali sneaks up behind me. I pull my hand back. I'm sure I have the guiltiest look right now.

"I'm sorry." I don't know what else to say. She scans my face, focusing on my lips, then back up to my eyes. My body tingles at her nearness and I take a step back.

"Do you play?"

What's she talking about? I decide to play it safe and assume she means the guitar. She leans past me and picks it up. I get a whiff of her hair and I have to bite back the appreciative groan on my tongue, threatening to embarrass me.

"Oh, no. I can't play any instruments or sing," I say.

"It's pretty easy. I can give you a quick lesson." She smiles at me. This time it's genuine. I shake my head no, but she continues. "There are only six strings. It can't be hard, right?

Six. That's it." She strums a few chords and I almost melt right in front of her.

I've never been this close to her playing. I take a step back to put distance between us and hope she doesn't see my goose bumps. Right now, I'm not at Camp Jacomo. I'm in a sunroom alone with Ali and she's playing for me. Perhaps we just had a light lunch and she's relaxing by playing a few new verses of a song she's working on. I'm doing that slip-away thing and a part of me wants to just let it happen, but the sane part holds me down and tells me to focus.

"I have very little rhythm." I'm surprised I can put a sentence together around her.

"Nah, I don't believe that. Everybody has rhythm. You just need to find it or find somebody who can bring it out in you."

We're both completely quiet and staring at one another. The wheels are spinning in my mind. I don't want to misinterpret her, but holy crap that was suggestive. Maybe she is just trying to be supportive about me dating again based on the conversation in the truck.

Our moment, if that's what it is, is ruined when the kids race back into the gazebo, excited to start singing again. I slip away, pretending to count heads when really I just need distance. They line up accordingly and Ali gets their attention by strumming her guitar.

Surprisingly, the kids sound good. Better than before. Maybe they just hate the silly camp songs, and I don't blame them. We end up with three songs for the bonfire tonight. I'm sure Ali would love to have them sing more, but we're limited on time. Since it's a talent show of sorts, other campers are going to show off whatever they want. Our concert will be last thing and the kids are excited to close it down. I just hope we don't run late because the smalls won't last.

Ali encourages the kids to create a group name so she can properly introduce them onstage. They immediately put their heads together and finally come up with the name Jacomo Jammers. They race off to the arts-and-craft area to make posters before the show.

"I think that went well," Ali says as we fold the chairs and stack them. I smile at her.

"You're good with kids. Do you have any?" I can't believe I just asked her that.

"Not yet, but I have a niece. This is so much easier than dealing with her. Something about family, you know?"

I don't know since I'm an only child. I nod because I don't know what else to say. Her response intrigues me. I wonder if she and her girlfriend are trying. Her children will be beautiful. We finish up, and I stand there not really knowing my role now that Ali's done with the kids. She grabs her guitar.

"It's not too late for that lesson," she says.

"Thanks, but I have to hit the kitchen and help with dinner," I lie. I'm sure Renee has covered my shift, but I need to get away from Ali. I don't want another awkward scene where I read too much into the situation.

❖

The bonfire night is always a good time. We roast hot dogs and marshmallows, and blast music so the kids can dance around until the talent show starts. Tonight I'm watching it from a distance. I fake a stomachache after dinner. I feel bad for missing out on the concert, but I need to get away for a bit. I know the more time I spend around Ali, the likelier I am to forget she's in a relationship. I don't need to do anything stupid so I hide in my cabin. I'm a coward. I have my laptop open, fingers on the keys, but I don't feel like writing. I don't feel like watching TV or reading or anything. I'm not tired so the only thing I do is think. Of course, Ali's on my mind. Why am I so intrigued by Ali Hart? Why her and not other women the past three years?

Truthfully, I've never felt this attracted to another woman before. I'm sure this isn't my sexual peak because I haven't had sex in forever. Does she also sense this attraction or is it just me? I sigh in frustration. I'm not getting anywhere. I shouldn't even be thinking about this because she has a girlfriend. I just feel so alive around her and a part of me is angry for that. I need to let this go. I need to find a way to get her out of my head. I want to give in and just have a quick fantasy where we have hot, sweaty sex, but I have a hard enough time being around her. If I start daydreaming about that now, I'll have to fake pneumonia and stay in my cabin until this weekend. I'll wait until she leaves before I give in to that temptation.

CHAPTER SIX

Friday night's movie is almost over by the time I arrive. I weave my way around sprawled bodies until I reach the kitchen. Saturday's breakfast is my responsibility. I forgot it was movie night. I'm juggling two grocery bags, and I just want to put what's in them away and get out. I don't want to distract anybody. If I'm really quiet, they won't pay attention to me.

"Where have you been all day and why are you all dressed up?" Rob asks. So much for my ninja speed and stealth. Now everybody is staring at me and I can feel the blush spread across my face. Wonderful. Several people are giving me the once-over. I'm wearing a white and blue summer dress with spaghetti straps and heels. My hair is piled high on top of my head, but pieces have fallen out. Five hours ago, I was pretty hot. The humidity has since shaken the curl out of my hair, and now I look like a hot mess.

"I just got back from dinner with my editor and his wife," I say as ten sets of eyes follow my every movement like cats tracking a beam of light. I'd offered to meet them for dinner because they're vacationing about seventy miles from camp. It's always nice to see Tom out of the office, and I simply love Patty. I also needed to get out of camp and away from the pull of Ali. One more day of her before my life goes back to the boring norm.

To be fair, I know this is a crush. Being around her and thinking about her constantly is just that. Maybe I read too much into the night in the fitness center and the day on the kitchen steps. Since then, she's been cordial and polite but still playful. Maybe that's just her. Maybe she's flirty. Or maybe I'm needy and it's time to get back out there. I feel like I'm already sabotaging myself before I even start dating again because I'm crushing on someone who's unavailable. Hot as hell and probably the sweetest woman on earth, but still unavailable. I busy my hands by putting up the groceries and trying my hardest to ignore everybody else in the room. I'm thinking about cutting away and discussing the power of prancing poetry with Em since I'm inspired after my conversation with Tom, but she and I agree that I need to stay focused on the task at hand. The sooner I put the food away, the sooner I can escape.

"Beth, we're getting ready to go to G2G in town. All of us. We need a break after this week," Val says.

"What's G2G?" Ali asks.

"It's this once-a-month lesbian celebration in Kansas City. They hold it in a large hall," Val tells Ali. "What do you say, Beth?"

"Thanks, guys, but no. I'm kind of tired." I'm not tired, but I don't want to drive an hour after just getting home. "Have fun. I'll see you in the morning." I almost run toward the front door just to get the out of there.

"Come on. Don't leave," Rob says.

I keep walking and waving until I'm down the stairs and headed for my cabin. I shut the door, strip down, and throw on my pajamas. My meeting with Tom has inspired me to continue writing. Since I'm trying something completely new by pouring out my ruined heart and torn soul, I take advantage of any downtime.

The laptop is balanced on my bare knees, and I'm sitting on the couch staring at the screen. My eyes keep wandering to the clock, and I'm wondering how the girls are doing. Truthfully, I'm wondering about Ali. Is she having fun? Is it even her scene? Does she get to have fun like this on her tour? I struggle between wanting to surprise them and staying here, but the pull of seeing their reaction to me showing up wins out. Something is blossoming inside me and I need to embrace it. I haven't felt giddy or playful in a long time. Maybe I'm ready to get out there and have fun again. Even if I don't meet anybody or talk to a woman outside of our group, at least I'm willing to try. I can't remember the last time I wanted attention from another woman. This crush is a short-lived, bright beacon that has found its way into my life. Ali is leaving tomorrow so it should be safe to be around her tonight. What could possibly happen in one night?

As I'm getting ready I finally recognize the feeling inside me. It's hope, perching on my soul. I smile. That's one of my favorites by Em. I'm excited as I get dressed. I find a pair of crisp, white linen slacks and a black silk tank that dips low to reveal a hint of my cleavage. Hello, ladies. I haven't shown them off in years. I pull my hair back in a messy French braid and style it so that it looks classy and windblown all at once. I know I'm attractive. I'm not always comfortable with my looks because the attention I've received hasn't always been positive. Tonight, though, I feel invincible.

The bar is dark and the parking lot is full of shadows I'm not entirely comfortable with. I spot Val's truck and the camp's SUV so I know everyone's inside. Suddenly, my confidence disappears. Do I go inside or get the hell out of here? Finally, I head for the door. As my eyes adjust, an overwhelming feeling of insecurity hits me as twenty women look me over at once. I smile and pick up the pace. Thankfully, I find the girls tucked in a dark corner. Obvious Ali fans surround one end of the table. I smile because even though I'm already annoyed with her fans, I've come up with a nickname for them that makes me giggle. I now will forever refer to them as elephants because the word sounds like Ali fans. Not very mature, but it'll get me through the night. My eyes meet Val's and I watch her spew beer and jump up from the table.

"Oh, my God! You're here! You're here!" She squeezes me. One day, I'm going to have to talk to her about her strength.

I hear cheers from the table as several counselors raise their longnecks to toast me. Only Val and Sandy know my history. The others just think I'm an introvert. Val drags me to the table and puts me on the other side of Sandy, two seats away from Ali. I don't think Ali even knows I'm here. Her back is turned and several women are asking her a ton of questions. I'm torn between listening to her conversation and allowing Val and Sandy to coddle me. I want both. I lean back in the chair, and even though I'm facing Val, I'm eavesdropping on Ali's conversation.

"As flattered as I am, I don't have the time right now. The tour keeps me busy," Ali says.

"But you must get lonely out on the road this long," the girl says. She gives Ali a look of longing. I roll my eyes, suddenly angry but trying to play it off. I know this happens a lot. I'm not famous like Ali is, but I do have a few fans out there who know that I'm gay and have wanted to hook up after book signings. I graciously turn them down, race to my hotel room, and hide under the covers.

"She's got a girlfriend, you know," one of the elephants tells the other one.

"Well, I used to have a girlfriend, but we broke up about three months ago," Ali says.

Forgetting about being discreet, I simply turn and stare open-mouthed at Ali. This entire week I thought she was in a relationship. That sure as hell would have been nice to be aware of on day one. I should know better than to believe everything I read online. If I hadn't stalked her, maybe this week's outcome would have been different. I hear the sympathetic cries of my poetic friends in my head.

"So what made you come out tonight? I'm so happy." Snatching me away from my imaginary support group, Val grabs me and presses her forehead to mine.

"Maybe it's time for me." I shrug, when in fact, it's been the hardest thing I've done in three years.

"You deserve happiness. It's been too long," she sighs into my hair. "Let's go have fun."

She grabs me by the hand and drags me onto the dance floor. I laugh at her attempts to make me laugh by dancing like a dork. She twirls and dips me, and, after three songs, I beg Val for a break. My shoes are killing me and I'm starting to sweat. We walk back to the table and a warm hand envelops mine. I follow the hand up and find myself staring at an attractive brunette with short brown hair and blue eyes. For a second, I'm bummed that it's not Ali. Wishful thinking. She smiles at me and I smile back.

"Why don't you stay for another song and dance with me?" she asks, pulling me closer to her so we can hear one another over the loud, thumping music. I tell her I need a break, but maybe later we can dance. I'm not nervous and I actually mean what I say, which surprises me. She isn't pushy, and in the ten seconds we speak, I find her charming. She reminds me of

Rachel Maddow. I feel a promising squeeze on my fingertips and she lets me slip away. I know I'm smiling, but I can't help it. It's a breakthrough.

"Why didn't you dance with her?" Val's practically yelling at me over the music, but the look on her face tells me she's proud.

"I just need a quick break. I'll dance with her later."

Val winks and kisses me on the cheek. I reach for an ice water to cool off and look around at all the women dancing and having a good time. I've missed this—the closeness and the camaraderie I share with these women. My iPhone vibrates on the table. I have a text message from an unknown number. I click on the text.

Dance?

I'm perplexed. For some reason, perhaps want, I turn to Ali and am met with a casual grin. Two thoughts enter my brain at once and I let them fight it out. How on earth did she get my number versus holy shit, Ali Hart just asked me to dance! My heart races and I can only respond with a slight nod. Just my luck—or maybe a higher being is answering my prayers—the music slows way down.

Ali stands up in the middle of a conversation with one of the elephants and reaches out. I hesitate for just a moment, staring at her long slender fingers, and prepare myself for the jolt. I can feel her heat even before our hands touch. Sliding my hand all the way into hers, I look into her eyes. They're dark and intense. This is a different Ali. This is a confident Ali. I'm torn between turning and bolting out the door and leaning into her, absorbing her heat. She grabs my hand and leads me to the dance floor. Her touch is firm and promising, and I feel like jelly.

"Is this okay?" she asks. She gently pulls me closer. I grit my teeth to keep them from chattering with a mixture of fear and anticipation. The curve of Ali's waist presses gently into my side, the softness of her breast brushes my collarbone. It's too much for me. I whimper and pray that she doesn't hear me. Not trusting my voice, I nod instead, knowing full well that everything is not okay. My body is flush with fever, yet my hands are cold and clammy. My heart beats in my lips and they swell with anticipation.

For a good five seconds, I give in to my temptation and drown myself in Ali. She smells like sandalwood and the sweetness of amaretto, her drink for the night. She is strong in my arms, solid and reassuring. Her muscles are tight, but her skin is soft and smooth. I can't tell if I'm hearing Ali hum with the music or if I can feel it through her body. Slowly, we're closing the gap, getting comfortable with each other. I close my eyes and will the crowd to disappear. I'm happy for about thirty seconds until a loud noise erupts through the club and I automatically try to pull away. Ali tightens her grip on me and pulls me closer. I moan as I crash into her and groan at my lack of control.

Britney, in a rush to get to the bathroom, has tipped over our table. Val and Sandy right it and scoop up our belongings before we cause any more of a scene. Ali and I race over there, our fingers still entwined. With regret, I pull away and follow Britney into the bathroom. She's hunched over the toilet and my heart goes out to her. She wasn't feeling the greatest all week because she caught something from one of the kids, and tonight was just too much for her. I help clean her up and we head back to our table.

"I'm going to take her back to camp," I say.

"No way. I'll do it," Val says. "You haven't been here that long. You should stay."

"Really, I'll take her. I need to leave now." I'm suddenly overcome with emotion.

Val hears the urgency in my voice and agrees.

"What can I do?" Ali asks. I so want to answer that with about a dozen inappropriate things, but I keep myself in check.

"Just hang out here and have a good time. Thanks for the dance." I follow Val, who's half dragging Britney to the car, and we help her into the passenger side.

"Bethy, I'm so sorry this happened," Val says, reaching out for a hug. "I'm happy you joined us."

"Believe it or not, I had a good time. Thanks for always nudging me to do things." I smile at her and climb into the Jeep.

"Ali's pretty great. You guys look good together," she says, giving me a look.

I try to play it off. "Ha ha. Very funny. She doesn't need my baggage. I'll see you later." I hurry up and get out of there before Val says anything else that requires a response. I've never been a good liar.

Thankfully, the hour drive back to the camp is pretty uneventful. Britney is quiet the entire trip and chooses to throw up after I get her out of the Jeep and almost to her cabin. I hold her hair and rub her back and wait until there's nothing left for her to puke up. I help her change clothes and get into bed. She wants to go to sleep, but I make her drink water and take two ibuprofen. That takes about five minutes. Most people think I'm very patient, but they don't know about my ability to tune everything out. Given the evening, I've been reciting Emily in between coaxing Britney to drink water and rubbing her back to relax her. She finally drinks enough to satisfy me and I tuck her in, but not before showing her the garbage can I place on the floor right by her head. I hose off the mess outside so nobody will step in it. I poke my head in and check on her one last time. She's snoring. On the way back to my cabin, I see headlights. Val and the counselors are back. I'm surprised. Val pulls up next to my Jeep.

"It just wasn't the same without you. We all wanted to leave." She shrugs.

"She's out cold." I thumb behind me at the cabin. "Thankfully, she waited until we stopped to get sick."

"Well, thanks for getting her back in one piece." Val waves good night to me and slowly drives off. Even though I know Ali's sitting beside Val, I avoid eye contact with her because I know I'll fall apart. I park my car and slip inside my cabin, knowing I'll have a hard time falling asleep. I will replay my night a thousand different ways, hoping for a different ending. I need to quit thinking about Ali and our dance. I sit down with my laptop and start typing words on the empty screen. Inevitably, the words become adjectives that describe either Ali or my feelings about her instead of anything worthwhile for the book. Passionate, caring, thoughtful, beautiful, considerate, warm, soft. I cross my arms and lean back in my chair. I'm getting absolutely nowhere. I take a deep breath and decide writing isn't the right thing for me now. I give up and resign myself to the couch, punching the remote and search for something to take my mind off Ali Hart.

CHAPTER SEVEN

Jogging is the best way for me to release pent-up emotions. When I simply run away, my mind clears. It's seven a.m. and my clothes are drenched in sweat. The humidity is so bad that I'm having a hard time breathing. I've jogged about three miles and decide it's enough. My demons are still going to be with me whether I jog a marathon or not. I'm constantly thinking about Ali and last night and things that I should have said and done differently. She's leaving this weekend, and I can't do much except suck it up and talk to her. I'm interested but afraid.

I head back to the cabin and cool down with a cold shower and a bottle of water. I put on a bikini so I can head to the secret, spring-fed pool after breakfast. It's a place the campers don't know about. It's not very big, but it's deliciously cold and just what I need. Saturday breakfasts are important around here to Renee, so hiding isn't an option. I pour a cup of coffee and suddenly a deep chill courses through my body. I look up from my notes on the counter and see Ali leaning against a post outside of my cabin. I freeze and stare at her for what feels like an hour, but is probably five seconds.

"Hi," I say, not able to move. The coffee cup is still halfway to my lips and I'm keeping it surprisingly steady.

"Hi. May I come in?"

I suddenly realize that I'm standing there in only a bikini, and I'm torn between opening the screen door and running into the bedroom for clothes.

"Ah, sure. Come on in and have a seat. I, um, I'm going to put some clothes on." I try not to run full speed back into the bedroom. I find a black swimsuit cover-up that will just have to do. It looks like a summer dress so I'm okay with it. I actually gasp at my reflection in the mirror. I haven't brushed my hair since I showered and it's a mess. I grab my brush and pull my hair back in a quick braid. My face is still flushed from my jog or from Ali's surprise visit. Or both.

"Sorry about that. Would you like some coffee?" I move about the kitchen looking for a purpose. I need to allow myself time to calm down.

"Yes, please. I saw you jogging so I knew you were up already. I want to talk if you have time," she says.

I'm completely surprised and nod. I really need to be better at communicating. I motion for Ali to sit on the couch and hand her a mug. I sit on the opposite side of the couch but turn to face her. I'm clutching my cup, my knuckles white against the blue porcelain. I force myself to relax.

"I think we got off on the wrong foot. I hope I didn't do anything to offend you or upset you. I have a feeling we would be great friends, but we've hardly talked."

I close my eyes. I'm in the climax of my own story. I feel like a character in one of my novels. This is my defining moment. "You're leaving today, right?"

"Today or tomorrow. I haven't really decided. Is it that bad?" Ali asks. Concern is etched on her face. I want to reach out and smooth away her worry, but instead I clutch my cup even tighter.

"No, no, no. I just want to make sure that if I'm completely wrong here, I only have to deal with it for another twenty-four hours."

"I just have to be in Nashville by tomorrow night," Ali says.

I take another deep breath and look Ali directly in the eye.

"I do want to get to know you better and be around you, but it's hard," I say. "It's a long story, but I haven't really wanted to get to know anybody for the last three years. When you showed up, I was completely drawn to you." Ali looks at me like I'm crazy. I sigh again. This is hard. "Up until last night, I thought you had a girlfriend and I had to keep my distance. It's hard enough to start dating again without falling for someone who's taken. Does that make sense?" I ask.

Ali stares at me. I stare back, trying hard not to shake. Finally, she speaks.

"Thanks for telling me. I realize it's not easy since we don't know each other. Yet." I perk up at that word. Oh, the power of words. If only she knew my obsession. She continues. "I wish I'd talked to you sooner. Gennifer, my ex-girlfriend, and I broke up three months ago, right before I went on tour. My schedule doesn't really allow me to meet new people. If you're up for it, I'd like to spend the day together."

I can't respond. I want to, but I sit there and stare at her. I want to jump up and squeal like a little girl, and in my mind that's exactly what I'm doing. Outwardly, I'm immobile.

"Or not," she adds.

"No, I think that sounds great," I finally say. I make a mental note to not always believe what I read on the Internet. I should know that by now after reading a ton of lies about myself.

"I like you, Beth. When I saw you, I knew I wanted to

get to know you. We don't have a lot of time left, but we can always make the most of it."

At that point, I'm ready to float away. I want to fly up and somersault in the air with pure joy. I try not to grin, but I can't help it.

"I'd like that." My voice sounds different, even to me. It sounds sultry. I want to excuse myself for a moment and do a happy dance in private.

The phone rings and it's Renee informing me that everybody's up and hungry. I almost groan at Renee's horrible timing. Just when this conversation is getting good. I tell her I'll be there in a few minutes.

"It's time for breakfast, and since I'm the chef this morning, I really need to get to the kitchen," I say. Ali smiles at me. My heart stops, then picks up speed, and I tell her she can go over there or wait a few minutes for me to throw on clothes.

I grab a pair of shorts and a white shirt and head for the bathroom. I'm not sure if Ali will still be waiting for me, so I dress in record time and bust into the living room. Ali's still here waiting, her back to me. I take the opportunity to get a really good, lustful look at her. She looks fantastic in linen shorts, a pale-pink button-down, and sandals. I can see the curve of her breasts and am reminded of last night when her body was pressed against mine. I recall her heat and scent and I'm rendered immobile again, lost in my memory of her. I'm totally staring when she turns and stares right back. I blush and head to the door, not really knowing what else to do.

"Umm, okay, let's go." I'm more nervous now than I was a few minutes ago. I'm completely embarrassed.

We arrive in the kitchen to find the six counselors who stayed behind this weekend, minus Britney, sitting around talking and drinking coffee. When they see me, they start giving me their breakfast requests, and I shush them playfully. Ali offers to help, but I insist that she join everybody else at the table. Putting me in charge of 400-degree burners with her near me is a bad idea. Cooking is another escape for me, and I don't want to burn myself or breakfast because she's standing a foot from me.

I whip up scrambled eggs and French toast. I skip the meat altogether and fry up tofu instead. Good nutrients, but not a whole lot of taste. I know that Ali is some level of vegetarian. I've been watching what she puts on her plate. Even during the BBQ, she ate only the sides. I'm happy that when I put the food out, she eats a little bit of everything.

"Is Britney okay?" Ali asks.

"She's still sleeping. She got up late, ate a few crackers, then crashed again. She did apologize for ruining our night," Val says.

"Well, I don't think our night was ruined. I had a great time," Ali says. I know she's looking at me. I can feel her stare, but I can't meet her gaze. My cheeks warm and my heart quickens.

"Ali, are you leaving us today or have you decided to stay until tomorrow?" Renee asks.

"I've decided to stay until the morning."

I can't help but smile.

"Great. What are your plans then for the day?" Renee asks.

Before I answer, Ali tells the group that I'm taking her on a quick hike and then swimming. I'm praying that nobody volunteers to go with us. Thankfully, and suspiciously, everybody else has plans, but that doesn't stop them from grilling Ali with questions.

I want to jump up and tell everybody to leave us alone

and let us start our daylong date, but I quietly sit there and try really hard not to roll my eyes.

"Well, go and have fun since Ali's time is limited," Renee tells us. "I've got the dishes."

I almost run for the door.

"How much time do you need to get ready?" I ask Ali. "You might want to wear something more casual. If we go hiking, I don't want to ruin your clothes."

"Give me fifteen minutes?"

"Sure. I'll meet you at your cabin."

We separate and I slow my fast walk down in case somebody's watching me. I can't appear too eager. Or at least I shouldn't. I really don't know what's going on here. I head for the bedroom to plan my wardrobe and finally settle on a one-piece bathing suit. My bikini is rather revealing, and I don't want Ali to get the wrong impression about me. This suit covers more, but I think it's still sexy because it's French-cut and reveals about as much cleavage as the bikini. I grab a pair of lightweight shorts and a Northwestern T-shirt. I braid my hair again. Riding in the open Jeep will mess it up, and this is the best solution to keep it back and out of my face. I throw water bottles, grapes, granola bars, and sunscreen in my backpack. I grab two towels and a blanket on my way out the door. I hop into the Jeep and head over to Ali's cabin with a minute or two to spare. Thankfully, she's outside waiting for me. She looks completely at ease and I feel like a total wreck. She smiles at me. That confident, sexy smile. I smile back and try not to shake.

"I brought my camera," she says. As much as I wanted to bring mine, I refrained. I don't want her to think I'm going to post a ton of pictures of us online. The Internet is my new archenemy.

"Cool. What kind is it?" I ask.

Ali hands me her little point-and-shoot. Our fingers briefly touch and I feel the jolt again. This time it's stronger. I feel the small calluses on the tips of her fingers from playing guitar, and the smoothness of her palm. I picture her hands touching my body, rough and soft against my skin. I try not to shiver but can't help it. I hope Ali doesn't notice. "This one's good." I'm a camera snob. I have seven cameras: four SLRs and three point-and-shoots.

"I like to take photos of the crowd when I'm playing. The fans go wild, and it's a good way to record my experience. It does a pretty good job."

The drive to the watering hole doesn't take very long. It's still early, and I ask Ali if she'd like to go on a hike first. She agrees, so I change course and park under some trees for the shade.

I find out that she loves hiking and spent several weeks last summer hiking Colorado and Wyoming. I share that I went to Arkansas last summer and explored caves with Val and Sandy.

"See? We already have a lot in common," Ali says.

"I don't doubt that." I grab the backpack and lead the way to the trailhead. I'm nervous with Ali behind me. I wonder if she's looking at me and if she likes what she sees. I'm not a girl who makes the first move. I'm reserved, but only because I don't like the unexpected.

"We lost a camper up here once for a few hours. Wait. I probably shouldn't have told you that," I say.

"I won't turn you in, but at least I have something to hold over you in case I want something from you."

This conversation turns sexual in my mind. It's apparent I need affection again, and soon. Ali must sense my discomfort.

"I know you're a great cook so maybe you'll have to cook me dinner tonight and I won't say anything to anybody about anything," she says.

"You're on." I'm happy that she appears to be completely innocent of the innuendo.

The path widens so we're able to walk side by side. I instinctively grab Ali when she trips twice on the path, our touch sending sparks throughout my body.

"I'm so clumsy today." Ali groans. "I normally don't need a seeing-eye friend."

That makes me laugh. I feel so alive around her, as if all my senses are heightened. I can smell the sharpness of the pines, the sweet sap clinging to the tree trunks, and Ali. She smells sweet and spicy like she did last night. I try not to lean too close for fear of getting caught, but I'm drawn to her. We climb on large, flat rocks to take a break, toasting with our water bottles. I don't know what's she's toasting, but I'm toasting my good luck.

"Here, scoot down closer to me," she says.

She takes her camera out and I'm both uncomfortable and elated. I try not to primp in front of her, like I'm cool with my sweaty look, but right now I'd sacrifice a small animal for a mirror and a brush, and for Ali to look the other way. Ali snaps the picture, then puts her hand up for me to stay put. She balances the camera on a nearby rock, focuses on me, and hits the timer. She jumps on the rock next to me. I have six more seconds of Ali's leg touching mine. I'm in heaven. At the last second, Ali casually puts her arm around my shoulder and I can't help but stiffen. This is a lot of contact for me and I'm completely unnerved. I can feel the heat of her across my back, and she's close enough that I can smell honey on her. She turns and smiles at me after the click of the camera breaks up our closeness. I desperately want to see the photo, but I decide to play it cool. She looks down at her camera and then back at me.

"You're beautiful," she says.

Now I'm completely derailed. I tell her thank you because I don't know how to handle her yet. It would seem silly to tell her the same thing even though I'm thinking it. We're having such a good time, and not just because she's saying nice things to me, but because I'm able to relax a little bit more around her. I wish we'd had our conversation days ago. We would have had more time to spend together and do fun things instead of having to cram a week's worth of getting to know each other in a single day.

Regardless, this is a perfect day. I love surrounding myself in nature. I always have. Ten months out of the year I live in Chicago, where people ignore one another and keep to themselves. These two months in the summer allow me to remember my roots and appreciate every day, especially today when I'm here with a beautiful woman. I look at my watch and decide we should go cool down at the watering hole. I'm already hot, and Ali must be dying with her long hair. Her face is already pink from the sun even though she put on sunscreen.

"Let's head back to the Jeep and I'll show you the best place at this camp," I say.

We're both sweating by the time we reach the Jeep. I feel wonderful though. We fall into a comfortable rhythm talking and learning each other's likes and dislikes. After spending two hours with her, I'm able to maintain eye contact better. A heaviness still hangs between us though. It weighs on my chest and squeezes my heart every time she slants her eyes at me or smiles. I don't know if she feels it, but I pretend she does. The drive is a short one and Ali is jumping out of the Jeep before I have it in park, excited to see the watering hole.

"This is beautiful." The watering hole is about the size of a pool and shaped like Texas. It's partially secluded by several trees that provide shade from the summer sun. "Why am I just learning about this now?"

"You've earned the right to this paradise." I wink at her, surprising myself with my blatant flirting. I turn away to put the backpack in a secure, dry place and stack the towels. When I turn back around, I see Ali peeling off her clothes to reveal a brown bikini. I stand there dumbfounded. The urge to touch her rushes back, and I tighten my hands into fists to keep from reaching out. Her stomach is flat and hard, just as I remember. Her legs are thin, but muscular, and her arms are strong and sinewy. She lets her hair out of the braid and acts as natural around me as if we've known each for years. I'm completely self-conscious at this point. "What happened to your bikini?" she asks.

"Well, I…ah, there really isn't much to it so I threw this one on instead. Why, is it bad?" I look down, hoping to God it isn't ripped or stained.

"Not at all." She smiles. "I just like the other one better." She dips her foot in and yelps, "This is cold!"

I'm still thinking about how she likes my bikini better. I'm doing that daydreaming thing again, and I know she's looking at me. I either need to say something or do something.

Feeling completely exposed, I dive in the water to get away from her for a moment. The cold stings but is refreshing at the same time. It instantly cools me from the heat of the sun and the heat of Ali. I surface to find Ali smiling at me.

"Come on in," I say.

Ali's pacing the side of the watering hole, as if she is hesitant to join me. She dips her foot in, then quickly pulls it out. I can't help but laugh.

"It'll be fine. It's not that bad, I promise."

She stares at me hard for a few seconds, then surprises me by diving right in. She surfaces about three feet from me and gasps. "It's cold!"

"But doesn't it feel great after our hike?" I ask.

She's treading water so close to me that sometimes our legs touch. I have to move away from her before I do something stupid and ruin this thin sliver of a relationship. I swim backward into a tiny alcove where I can stand up. Ali follows me. She's moving toward me, quietly and persistently. I must have a look of sheer panic on my face because she stops and speaks very softly.

"Please don't be nervous around me." Her voice is low and sensual.

I don't know what to say, so I stare back at her. I watch her inch closer to me. Her pace slows, but her course is constant. I finally find my voice.

"I can't help it." Really? That's the best I can come up with? I shake my head at myself.

I'm finally as far back as I can go without actually climbing out of the watering hole. I wonder how she's so confident. I'm shaking wondering what's going to happen next and she seems totally calm. I lick my lips when she's about two feet away and she grins. She reaches out and touches my hair.

"I've wanted to do that for a while now. I love long, thick hair and yours is such a beautiful color," she says, twirling the end of my braid slowly between her fingers. She pulls on it, bringing me closer to her. "And I've wanted to do this for a while, too," she says, right before her lips touch mine.

I'm afraid to move, afraid that if I do, this dream will disappear. Her lips are smooth and warm. She runs her tongue over my lower lip and pulls it inside her mouth to gently suck it. Her hands are on my face, holding me close. Something inside me breaks and a rush of warmth courses through my body. I close the small gap between us and deepen the kiss. Her body is hard against mine. I wrap my arms around her neck while she runs her hands down my side. Her fingers press firmly into my waist.

"Are you guys up here?"

I quickly pull away from Ali. We're both breathing heavily, and it's going to be obvious to anybody what we were doing. I can feel my heartbeat pulsing in my swollen lips. I can see passion in Ali's eyes. I know we're busted. A part of me doesn't care, but the other part wants to keep this a secret a little longer.

"We're in the pool!" I yell. My eyes never leave Ali's face.

Ali ducks under the water when Rob rounds the corner, leaving me to deal with him by myself. Before I have a chance to try to come up with something to say, she surfaces, laughing.

"You should have told me about this place sooner," she tells Rob.

"I'm sorry. I came up here to let you know that you got a delivery from UPS. I thought it was probably important because it's Saturday," he says. He starts taking off his shirt and kicking off his shoes, clearly anxious to join us. Ali smiles at him and thanks him for delivering the message.

I want to kill him. He jumps in and swims around Ali. I take a moment to collect myself. At least I know Ali's interested in me. Now how am I going to get rid of Rob? As much as I love him, I really don't like him at this moment. I only have a few precious hours left with Ali, and I really want her to myself. Not wanting to pout, I swim over to them. Rob's talking about all of the concerts he's been to, and Ali's being sweet answering all of his questions. It sounds like, even though Ali considers herself a folk artist, she's sung with some impressive mainstream singers. I can tell she's getting somewhat overwhelmed and I step in.

"Give her a break, Rob. She's on vacation, not an interview."

"So, what are you girls doing this afternoon? I'm bored," he says. It's obvious he wants to hang out with us. No way in hell am I going to let that happen. Apparently, he didn't get the memo at breakfast this morning with the others. I'm not sure how to tell him to get lost, but I will somehow.

"Beth's going to show me how to work a camera, and we're going to look at some photos," Ali says.

I love the way Ali says my name. It almost sounds breathless. I'm hoping that her explanation of our day doesn't sound like fun to him. I'm right. He shows no interest and continues swimming in the pool. I want to smile, but I'm trying to stay cool. I climb out of the pool and grab a towel to dry off. I'm hoping Ali gets the hint so we can ditch Rob before he suddenly wants to become the next Ansel Adams and needs photography tips. I dry off slowly because I can feel Ali watching me. I have some kind of connection with this woman, and my body crackles with energy whenever she's near.

"I guess I'll join Beth," Ali tells Rob. She swims over to me. I hand her a towel and watch her dry off. She's very graceful and she flows. I can't explain it any better than that. Her movements are fluid and smooth, so very different from my own. I close my eyes for a long moment, savoring her nearness. When I open them, Ali's looking at me, her eyes narrow with passion. She doesn't say a word. We gather up our stuff in silence, wave good-bye to Rob, and head back to the Jeep. I need to break the tension between us. Even though it's a good tension, it still weighs on me, and I try to lighten the mood.

"What do you want to do now?" I ask Ali. As much as I want to throw myself at her, I know it's probably not a good idea.

"I liked what we were doing back there, but I'm starting to understand that privacy isn't big here. Let's try to find another place."

My mind's racing through the camp, trying to find secluded places, and I decide on the big maple tree in the meadow. I want to pick up where we left off so I find the closest place to where we are. Ali smiles at me and my teeth chatter. I steal glances at her as we drive to the meadow. She's truly thrown me off my axis. My mind is full of words that have to come out, but I have no idea where to start. I want to yell, scream, whisper all of the emotions that threaten to bubble over, but I can't put words to these feelings. Maybe Ali doesn't need a lot of words. I know I wear my heart on my sleeve. Forget me in a game of poker. I'm worthless. Ali seems like a cool cat. Very together. After I park the Jeep, I reach for the backpack again and hand Ali the blanket. She lifts her eyebrow at me and I blush.

"I was here the other day, and trust me, the ground is hard and dry and we'll need the cushion," I say.

Ali winks. I wish I had her confidence. We walk over to the tree trunk and unfold the blanket so it's completely in the shade. I set up a mini picnic while Ali braids her hair back. I want to sink my fingers into her silky hair or at least help her braid it. Instead, I rearrange the food over and over again until realize I must look OCD.

"So tell me about yourself," Ali says, grabbing a handful of grapes. She leans back on her elbows, and it takes all of my willpower to maintain eye contact and not allow my eyes to wander over her body. Instead, I make the mistake of watching Ali's mouth and almost lose it. One of my secret turn-ons is kissing with food. There's something sensuous about licking chocolate cake from the corners of a warm mouth or sharing a bite of fruit. I get lost in Ali for a moment, then decide it's probably wise to answer her.

"There's not much to tell. I'm a writer, I live in Chicago, but I'm a Kansas City Chiefs fan," I say.

"I'm sure there's more to you than that. Tell me about your family. Tell me about what you do when you aren't writing, and tell me why you're single." That catches me off guard. I really don't like to talk about my bad breakup with anybody, let alone somebody I'm interested in. I've kept that part of my life bottled up so long I'm not sure how to tell the story. How do you inform somebody new in your life that your partner of five years simply walked out on you? It's a scar that's just starting to heal. I'm not in the mood to pick at it, but Ali deserves to know.

"I'm an only child. My parents are retired and live in Texas. I have an uncle in Illinois near Chicago, so that's nice. I like to jog, read, play word games with random people, and I'm single because my partner decided to leave me for another doctor in her practice."

There. It's out. My confession is surprisingly easy.

"Wow. She's stupid," Ali says.

I burst out laughing. That isn't the reaction I expected from her. It makes me feel good though, and a wave of relief washes over me. My body shakes with the freedom of my admission. I relax. A silence settles between us as we both process that information. I know that everybody breaks up with someone. My story has been told millions of times before. It's just hard to move on when you have nowhere to go.

"Can I ask you a question?" Ali turns to me.

Shit. I thought we were done with this. I nod.

"Why do you only play word games with strangers?"

she asks. I smile. Ali is perfect. I want to kiss her again. "I'm pretty good at Words with Friends. You should start playing me. I mean, I don't have a degree in English, but I think I'm pretty good." Ali nudges me with her shoulder.

"Thank you," I say.

She nods. "You know what?"

I tense up and look around, thinking someone else has found us. "What?" I ask.

"It appears we are the only ones here." Ali leans up close to me. She slides her hand up to my neck and gently pulls me down to her mouth. I feel the softness of her lips and melt into her. I'm desperately trying not to appear eager and pounce on her, but it's so hard with her lips on mine. She's a fantastic kisser. I want to push her down and slide across her body, full contact from head to toe, but I refrain. Another time, another place. It's too early for that, and I don't want Ali's opinion of me to change. I break the kiss and sigh.

"So what do we do now?" I ask her. I'm looking at her neck and I want to suck on it, taste her, smell her. My body swells. I need to slow my thoughts and wants down. I swear she can read my mind because she gives me a smile that is incredibly sexy, very different from her other smiles.

"I suggest we spend as much time together as we can," she says.

"That's going to be hard since you're leaving this weekend." I break eye contact.

"I'll have some time off here in a few weeks, and I'd love to see you then. That is, if you want to and can get away. And you're always more than welcome to come see me on the road."

I know that I'm going to do everything I can to see her onstage. I don't know her music, really, but I'm determined to be familiar with every one of her songs before I see her concert. "I'm sure we can work something out. I'd love to see you on tour."

Ali is very close to me. I'm so nervous my stomach is trembling. I decide we need to get moving before she can see how much she's affecting me. I don't know if I'm ready for this.

"We should probably get out of this heat. Want to go back to camp?" I swear Ali sighs, but she helps me pack up and I wonder if I've made a mistake. It's obvious she wants to kiss and God only knows what else. I'm positive she's used to getting her way with women, but I can barely handle kissing her. This is too fresh for me. I don't want Ali Hart to be my rebound girl, even if it has been three long, lonely years. We head for the Jeep and see Renee waiting for us.

"There you two are. I've been looking for you. Ali, we'd love to have a small dinner tonight as a way of saying thank you for everything you've done this week. We promise not to keep you up late," Renee says. There goes my plan for an intimate dinner.

"That sounds great, Renee," Ali says. I notice hesitation on her part. Perhaps she's hoping I'll rescue her and tell Renee about our tentative dinner plans. She doesn't know that I'll roll over for Renee any day of the week. She's one of the strong ones who helped me through my breakup. She picked me up, kissed my boo-boos, and kicked me in the ass when I needed to quit feeling sorry for myself. If Renee wants dinner with Ali, she'll get dinner with Ali without my interference. We pick a time and Renee leaves us alone.

I turn to Ali and she's leaning back in the seat, her eyes closed for a moment. I take a mental picture to pull out later. She looks so young and peaceful, and my heart goes out to her because her life is going to pick up full force tomorrow as she heads out to continue her tour.

"Do you mind if I grab a quick shower? Then if you're up for it, I can come over for a bit until dinner," she asks. This snaps me back to reality.

"Sure," I say. When I drop her off I remind myself to settle down. Ali shoots me a heart-stopping smile, and I have to grip the steering wheel to keep from following her. I drive over to my cabin and race up the stairs, anxious to clean up. My life has changed so much in just a few short hours. Something good is happening here, and I just hope that it snowballs into something bigger and better. I look around my cabin, happy that I don't have to clean it very much. I jump in the shower and wince at the sunburn on my neck and face. I hope Ali's in better shape. I slip into a pair of capris and a long tank top. I need to wear something light against my warm skin. Leaving my hair down to air-dry, I head out of the cabin to wait for Ali.

"Hi. I didn't want to scare you by busting in your cabin, so I decided to wait out here," Ali says. She's on the porch swing, her long legs tucked underneath her, and her right arm stretched along the back of the bench. She looks completely relaxed again. Her hair's down and still wet. I'm surprised to see that it's naturally wavy. She's wearing cut-off jeans and a form-fitting red plaid shirt with sleeves to her elbows. She looks like a cowgirl. I want to walk over to her and kiss her, but instead I scold her.

"Come inside. I think we've been out in the sun long enough today." I look at her to make sure she isn't pink like me, allowing myself to quickly imagine Ali without tan lines, then push the thought back into my mind to pull out at a later date. She follows me and I offer her something cool to drink.

"Whatever you're having." She thanks me and takes a seat on the couch, more in the middle than on one side or the other. I sit next to her, but on the side that gives us more space.

A part of me knows she's testing me, but this is a big step for me and she's just going to have to be patient.

"Am I keeping you from writing?" she asks. I want to laugh at her. Even if I am struck with the strongest inspiration I've ever felt in my life, there's no way I'm leaving this couch.

"Not at all. I usually do that at night anyway. I don't have the distraction of the kids or the camp. It's very quiet around here then."

"What made you become a writer, Beth?" There it is again. The breathy way she says my name. I clench my glass to keep my hands from trembling. Now that I've touched her, I want more. I think about how soft her wet body felt against mine, and I'm anxious to touch her again. I shake the thoughts from my head and focus on Ali's question instead.

I'm tempted to recite Emily right now and her fascination with books and the journeys they inspire, but I don't know if that will seem crazy to Ali. I can practically see Emily, hands clasped in front of her face, leaning toward me, beaming with delight.

"I learned to read when I was young, and I loved the adventures I'd go on with the characters. As a kid, I wasn't exposed to a lot, but a book could take me anywhere. I just loved that, and I decided that I wanted to write to help people escape. I didn't do well as a children's author, but I'm doing okay as an adult book—wait. Not 'adult book,' but a book geared toward adults instead of kids."

Ali chuckles. "I know what you mean. I'm going to have to pick up one of your books. Pretty much all I do on the road is read. Which one do you recommend first?" Ali asks. I can't help but smile. Ali Hart wants to read my books!

"My first book, *The Nearness of You*, is probably a good start. It's a story about a woman who becomes obsessed with a man who works in her building. He ends up dead—"

"No!" Ali clamps her hand over my mouth. "Don't ruin it for me! I want to figure it out for myself." She's close to me again. I can see the caramel flecks in her eyes. Her eyes are actually a dark copper color instead of dark brown. She slowly moves her hand away and I lick my lips. I can taste the salt of her skin and smell the honey in her lotion. I have a choice. I can lean forward and kiss her, or I can say something to break the tension and lean back. For some reason, perhaps idiocy, I speak instead of sinking into her.

"I'm sure you'll figure it out. I just hope you enjoy it. It's like every other murder mystery out there. Except I wrote it." And just like that, the mood is broken. Ali leans back, and I see something in her eyes that looks like regret. I try to convince myself that going slow is the answer, but I don't even know if I believe that. Maybe Ali just wants to have one night together. She doesn't strike me as a love-'em-and-leave-'em kind of girl, but I really don't know her. I fantasize that she'll wait forever for me, if that's how long it takes. Logically, I know she won't, and I don't want her to. She's too beautiful not to touch.

"So now that I've told you about why I became a writer, tell me why you became a singer." I need Ali to talk because I can't stop trembling.

"I've always loved music. When I was three or four, we visited one of my mom's friends who had a piano in her dining room. It completely fascinated me. I wanted to touch it, but my mom wouldn't let me. I sat down and threw the biggest tantrum. Finally, my mom's friend picked me up and played 'Old MacDonald Had a Farm' for me, and I reached down and played the song almost perfectly. I knew I did something right because she bought me a keyboard that day. It was only a month or two before I had my first piano."

"You're a child prodigy." I love stories like this.

Everybody is good at something, and it's always interesting to hear about.

"Not really," Ali says. "I still have a hard time reading music. I normally play by ear."

"Did you study music in college?" I ask, then regret the question. Not all successful people have degrees.

"Yeah, at Mount Holyoke. They have a really good music program and it was pretty close to home. It's an all-girls school so that helped me decide to attend," she says. I laugh at her explanation.

I'm starting to relax again around Ali. It's still hard to maintain eye contact because sometimes she sends me a look that shakes me to the core. It's not a suggestive look, just a fire that flares up and sends tiny jolts of what-ifs throughout my body. What if we start kissing now? What if I reach out for Ali? What if we remove the pillows that separate us on the couch? What if I tell Ali to kiss me again? I'm getting lost in her. I'm studying her mouth, not entirely paying attention to the words coming out. Her lips are full, and I imagine biting and nipping and soothing them against my tongue. They're so naturally red. I believe that the redder the lips, the more sensitive they are. But maybe that's just my fantasy. Either way, they completely fascinate me. The curves in the corners of Ali's mouth make me want to lean forward and run my tongue across her lips until she moans for a hard kiss.

"And if you keep looking at me like that..." When the words finally sink in, I look up at Ali in shock. Not only do I take my mind away from situations and talk to poets in my head, but sometimes I completely forget I'm in the middle of a conversation. If I could have any super power, it'd be the ability to stop time just so I could finish my thoughts before continuing conversations. I like being under the radar. Well, except in situations like this. I'm thankful I have a sunburn because I know that my face is bright red.

"I'm sorry. I didn't mean to…I'm sorry," I say.

Ali squeezes my hand gently. "I'm just teasing. You just have this faraway look, and I know you disappeared there for a minute."

"I'm normally not this thrown off." I focus my attention back on Ali's face, trying hard not to notice how her eyes sparkle or how her long fingers are casually twisting her chestnut-colored hair. Ali shoots me a lazy smile but thankfully doesn't call me out. Again.

"I'm sorry I wasted time," I say. Judging by the look on her face, my confession surprises her.

"It wasn't a waste. You were protecting yourself so I understand. I just figured you didn't like me for some reason. Maybe you don't like musicians or maybe I was rude around you or something. I'm not always aware of my actions, and sometimes my guard does slip," she says.

"Oh, no. You've been perfect. Really. I just was being selfish and stupid." I'm just so glad that Ali took the time to make the first step. I'm too much of a coward.

❖

Darren's busy grilling veggie kabobs marinated in a garlic-and-herb seasoning that smells heavenly. Renee has whipped up potatoes and made black-skillet biscuits. A tray of fresh fruit and cheese and two bottles of wine are already on the table.

"Oh, you did too much," Ali says.

Renee gives her a quick one-arm hug and reassures her that this is our way of saying thanks.

"I've really enjoyed myself so much. Thanks again for having me," Ali says.

I stand next to Ali, close enough to reach out and touch her if I want. I can't believe she's leaving early in the morning. I can't believe I wasted six precious days.

"So what made you start this camp?" Ali asks Renee.

"Well, one of our nieces had a hard time in school with being gay. I saw her struggles early on and decided there needed to be a place where she and her friends could go and not worry about being bullied or hated. We've been around for years, and I plan to keep this place until I die," Renee says. She opens up one of the bottles of wine and fills four glasses. "We had some struggles at first with the town approving zoning and other stuff, but once they got to know us and understood our goal, they were supportive. We still get the occasional hate stares and slurs flung our way, but we do bring business to town, and most of the townies who don't like us simply ignore us."

"Your family must be proud of what you're doing here. Especially your niece. You've made a significant change to support your family. I think it's great. What does she think?" Ali asks. At this point, I'm tempted to knock over my glass of wine for attention so that I can change the subject. This is not something I want to discuss or hear right now. I grit my teeth and hang on. This is about to get awkward.

"She thinks it's wonderful. She worked at the camp during her summers in college and a few years after that, but then she got busy with her career. She helps us by providing scholarships for some of the children who can't afford it, so even though she isn't here, she still is a strong supporter," she says.

"Where is she now?" Ali asks. I freeze, and Renee starts fidgeting with the tablecloth. Apparently, she realizes that this conversation has gone too far. There's no way out.

"She's down in Memphis. She has a practice down there," Renee says.

Ali looks at me. "Didn't you live in Memphis for a few years?"

I so want to die right now.

Before I can answer, Renee does. "I don't know if Bethany told you, but we got to know her because she was our niece's partner."

CHAPTER EIGHT

I'm sorry I didn't mention Crystal before. I thought Renee might have said something."

"That is quite a surprise," Ali says. We are slowly walking back toward the cabins. "I guess I didn't realize your connection here. I just thought you volunteered during the summers."

"Crystal and I came out here every summer during the five years we were together. She's busy with her practice now, and so I come out and help when I can," I say. I shrug like it isn't a big deal, but Ali picks up on my discomfort and changes the subject.

"Well, I guess we're here," she says. We walk up the steps to her cabin. "Would you like to come in for a bit?"

Yes, of course! I want to yell, but instead I shake my head no.

"I'd love to, but you need to get up early. It's not going to be an easy drive for you tomorrow. And it's already eleven." I look at my watch.

"Eleven isn't late," she says. She pouts her lips. I think she's adorable.

"I'm sure it's not for you, but eight gets here early and you probably still need to pack and load up your car, right?" I ask. She laughs, nodding.

"Yeah, you're right. Thanks for spending time with me today, Bethany. It was my favorite day at Camp Jacomo." She winks at me. My heart flutters and I reach out to hold the railing. I think if I don't, I might float away just from the look in her eyes. I can't help but smile.

"It was a pretty good day, wasn't it?" I say.

She answers me with a warm kiss. It takes me by surprise and melts me all at once. She wraps her arms around me and gently pulls me closer. I want more. Ali breaks the kiss right then, much to my dismay, and turns to climb the stairs.

"Thank you for escorting me, fair maiden," she says. She swoops into a low bow, causing me to smile again. "Hopefully, I'll see you before I leave," she says.

I want to stay, but I need to go. I continue with the charade and curtsey back.

"Most definitely, kind lady."

"Good night! Good night! Parting is such sweet sorrow," she says. Giving me a quick wink, she disappears behind the door.

I laugh. Ali just quoted Shakespeare. She's turning out to be perfect. I head back to my cabin with my fingers over my lips, trying to keep the feel of Ali's warmth against me.

CHAPTER NINE

It's seven forty-five and I'm trying hard not to pace around Renee's kitchen. What's taking Ali so long? I busy myself with the dishes and turn when I hear Renee speak.

"I wasn't sure if you were up yet or not, but I was about ready to send Bethany down to make sure you were awake. I know you need to get on the road," she says.

Shit. I couldn't come up with a single reason to go to her cabin this morning. I should have thought of that one. I smile at her and she grins. It's a private grin, different than the one she shoots Renee and Darren.

"How did you sleep?" Renee asks Ali.

"I could have slept longer, but I feel fine," she answers.

I didn't sleep well. I didn't sleep at all, actually. I tossed and turned, thinking about Ali. I couldn't sleep so I wrote. All night. The problem with not sleeping is that you start second-guessing everything and your judgment is severely impaired. Hence, the success of infomercials at three a.m.

Renee is still talking to Ali and I take a moment to think about our relationship. What if Ali drives away and I never hear from her again? I run down my list of what-ifs again, but they aren't as exciting as the ones from last night. I frown and notice Ali is looking at me. I shake my head to let her know it's nothing.

"We made pancakes and Bethany ran to the farmer's market first thing this morning to pick up some fruit," Renee says.

"What time did you get up this morning?" Ali asks me.

"Umm…I haven't really gone to bed yet." I quickly explain before Ali or anybody can scold me. "But I'll sleep when you leave. I usually do on Sundays anyway." I can feel Ali staring at me.

"So what did you do last night?" Ali asks. She gives me a wicked grin and raises her eyebrow at me.

"I wrote." I grab the fruit I just cut and set it on the table. I really wanted to hang out with Ali all night, but she does have a stupid drive ahead of her, and it wouldn't have been fair of me to keep her up for my own selfish reasons.

"Can you write whenever or just when you're inspired? Did you have an inspirational day yesterday?" she asks. Her voice is flirtatious, almost as if she is challenging me to talk about our date in front of Renee and Darren. I decide to flirt back.

"Oh, definitely when I'm inspired," I say. I can tell I've surprised her and she nods.

"That's really good to know. Well, I hope you finish your manuscript soon. I'm excited to start reading your books." Ali smiles at me as she slides into her chair.

"Her books are fantastic. You'll really enjoy them," Darren says. "Every so often she throws a twist in and the stories really make you think. I love them."

I can feel my cheeks burning as everybody in the room looks at me.

"Hey. Don't give anything away." Renee smacks his shoulder. She sits on one side of Darren and I'm forced to sit right across from Ali. Ali looks at me smugly and I can't help but grin back at her. At least I can look at her and not worry about getting caught staring.

We spend most of breakfast talking about the rest of Ali's tour. Her upcoming schedule is intense with very few breaks. She seems happy though.

"What was your favorite part of the week?" Renee asks Ali.

"The people. Everybody treated me like I was one of them. It's nice to be Ali Hart, choir teacher, not Ali Hart, musician," she says.

"It's been our pleasure. Now please don't take this the wrong way, but it's getting late and you need to get on the road." Renee points at the clock. It's eight forty-five already.

Ali offers to clean up, but Renee shoos her away.

"Give me a hug. I've packed a lunch in case you don't want to stop," Renee says. She hugs Ali and hands her a large basket. Ali holds it up and we all laugh. I can't imagine what Renee packed in there.

"Thank you. I'm sure it's delicious," she says. "Will you help me load my car, Beth?" she asks.

"I can help you with that," Darren says. He's halfway to the door before Renee shoots him a deadly look. "Actually, Beth can help you. I forgot I need to do something very important for Renee." He says good-bye to Ali and quickly disappears. The angelic look on Renee's face doesn't fool me. She ignores me and tells Ali good-bye again.

We head toward her cabin, walking very slow, preserving our last few minutes together.

"I can't believe you've been up all night. You look great," she says. She nudges me with her shoulder. "Did you get a lot written?"

I look up at her and shrug. "Eh. I did all right."

"If you'd said no, I would've asked why you didn't come back over."

I freeze and almost stumble. That was an invitation.

"You needed sleep because you've got a long drive and an even longer night," I say. I did think about going back to her cabin about nine hundred times throughout the night.

"Thanks for looking out for me." Charming Ali is back. I sigh with relief. She must not realize how hard this is for me. We reach the cabin, and as much as I want to stall just to be near her, I know she needs to get going.

"I only have a few bags and my guitar," she says.

"Then I guess you don't need my help," I say. I playfully turn to leave. Ali grabs my hand and pulls me back to her. I want to smile at her, but I don't because she has a very serious look. She brushes her fingers along the side of my cheek and down to my neck. She looks at me and I lick my lips, waiting. I want her to kiss me. I am incredibly turned on simply by her touch.

"Of course I need your help," she says softly. "I'm hoping you'll keep me from dying of boredom on the road."

I know this is her way of asking me if I'm interested in pursuing this past five minutes from now. She's still touching me and she's waiting. She wants my decision. Time to be bold. I kiss her softly at first, forgetting and remembering how soft her lips are. She tastes like syrup and I want more. I move closer. This time the kiss is deeper and I slide my hands up to her shoulders. Every part of her body that I have touched is soft. She is so smooth, and I'm overcome with an urge to bite her. I don't know why, but I'll worry about that desire later. Right now, I need to taste her and feel my body against hers. I moan the second her body touches mine. I've forgotten how wonderful a woman feels. How soft she is and how her curves seem to mold with mine. Ali fits me like a puzzle piece.

She slows the kiss down and we break apart, both of us slightly panting. Okay, I'm severely short of breath, but I can't let her know that, so I try to cover it up by looking down and taking deep breaths. We both just stand there. I'm surprised Ali is quiet. She's the big flirt, and right now, her silence is golden. I kind of like throwing Ali off her game. She leans down and kisses me again, quick and softly. "Mmm. I certainly wish I had more time for that," she says. And now she's flirty again. "I don't want to, but I really need to go."

I nod, but I don't say anything. I still can't talk. I've caught my breath, but now I don't know what to say. I help her with her bags, but I don't touch her guitar. It's in a soft case and I'm afraid I would break it. I've already pictured myself tripping down the stairs and crushing it. Or banging it on the side of the car, or scratching it on the cabin door or post. Nope, I'm going to let her carry it.

"Get some sleep, okay? I'll talk to you soon," she says. She turns to me for a quick hug. I brace myself for the contact, reveling in her warmth. She smells good, feels good, and a big part of me is regretting not visiting her last night. I hug her for a little bit longer than socially acceptable and pull away when I feel her smile in my hair.

"I'll talk to you soon. Be safe." I found my voice! I watch Ali drive off and can't help but wonder what's going to happen with us. We have such different lives, but so much in common, too. Not that all relationships are predetermined, but this one is so completely different than anything I've experienced before. I'm suddenly very nervous about the outcome.

CHAPTER TEN

Time has stopped since Ali left eight days ago. Why does it feel like four months? We have been communicating via phone calls and text messages since the day she left. She seems excited to talk to me, but we really haven't had a lot of time. I know that I'm opening up to her, and I can't stop this want no matter how hard I try. My attraction to Ali is powerful and raw.

"It's good to see you out and about with a smile on your face, Beth," Renee says. She's looking at me intently, silently prodding me for information. We're hiking with a handful of campers, but we're trailing the pack so we can speak in private.

"Yeah, I've been pretty happy this week," I say. It appears that she already knows why. Strangely, it doesn't bother me that Renee is Crystal's aunt. I think we're closer than she and Crystal.

"It's Ali," she says.

"We had a good weekend before she left and we've kept in contact," I say. I shrug, but we both know this is a giant step for me.

"I like her a lot. She's wonderful and I knew you'd get along. You both are beautiful and smart women," she says. I nod a thank you.

"I might go see her July Fourth weekend down at the Lake of the Ozarks. She has a few days off during the tour, and her aunt and uncle own a lake house." Renee doesn't say anything, just puts her arm around my shoulders and squeezes. "It feels good again, you know? I just hope that I don't screw it up or get screwed in the process." I've got to give Robert credit for pushing me to go for it. He's definitely more in tune with my daring side and going for it than Em is.

"Just let things happen naturally. Do what you need to do for you. If you want this and you think this will make you happy, then go for it," she says.

"I don't know what's going to happen. We couldn't be more opposite. She's on the road a lot and I like to stay at home and write. She performs for other people all the time and I'm fine not being the center of attention. But I've never been this drawn to another person before. It's scary. I don't know if I'm this excited because it's been so long for me, or if we really do have a connection," I say.

"So what happened last weekend?"

"We only kissed, but it was so nice." I take a moment to relive our first kiss. What a great first kiss. Possibly the best. "I'm just a wreck around her all the time. Even on the phone. I can't be calm. It's like I'm an awkward, klutzy teenager again. It's embarrassing."

"When Darren and I started dating, we were both that way. He almost burned down his dining room trying to light candles. He knocked over the candle and it lit a napkin on fire. The napkin lit the tablecloth and we were racing around trying to put it out and it was so chaotic but perfect all at the same time," Renee says. She laughs. "We shared our first kiss in that smoky dining room."

"You two are so happy together. I hope I can have that kind of relationship."

"I'm sure you will, doll. You have too much to give to somebody, and I can't imagine you not getting snatched up in a heartbeat. You just need to let go of the past and focus on the possibilities of your future," Renee says. She's so smart. I always go to her for advice. She's Dr. Phil, Oprah, Suze Orman, and Aunt Bee all rolled up into one.

The hike ends about noon and the counselors march the kids to the lunch hall and I'm able to make my escape. I left my phone in my cabin because I knew if I took it on the hike, I would be on it the entire time. I have four text messages from Ali. They're lighthearted and fun. The last one is a photo of Ali and a cow. The bus stopped to fix a flat, and Ali had Brian take a photo next to a very friendly cow. It makes me laugh out loud. I text her back.

Looks like you're having more fun than me. Who's your new friend?

Ali texts me almost immediately.

Do you have time to talk now?

I call her. I have her number already stored in my favorites and memorized. All ten digits and I'm horrible with numbers.

"Hi! Looks like you're having a crazy, busy day so far." I can't keep the giddiness from my voice. I roll my eyes.

"It's definitely been crazy. We're a little bit behind schedule, but we'll be fine. How are you? Did you get any sleep?" she asks.

"I slept about five hours. I got up early and went on a hike with Renee, Val, Rob, and a ton of kids. They needed an extra body. We actually walked the trail that you and I hiked."

"That was a great hike. I took a lot of pics that day. It's

the only photo I have of you. You should email me more," she says. I cringe. I hate having my picture taken. I would much rather be behind the lens than in front of it.

"I can probably send you something later today," I say. We talk for about ten more minutes, and, by the time we hang up, I'm completely stressed about what photos to send her. I don't have anything recent. If I ask an adult, they will question me and I'm still not ready to share. I don't want to ask Renee. That would be weird. Looks like I'm going to have to bribe a camper to take my picture. I grab my camera and head out, snapping random photos of the camp. I see Matthew, Ali's favorite camper, and grab him. I tell him I want to send a photo of us to Ali. He agrees and we set the timer on the camera and snap a bunch of photos together, some silly, some serious, and some normal. Phew. I think I also have a photo from one of my book covers that we never used hidden somewhere on my laptop. I can probably send that because I haven't changed much since last fall. Except for the suntan.

I open my email to send Ali a message when I see that she has sent me an email. The subject line says Missing You. When I click on it, my stomach flutters and my heart jumps. It's a picture of Ali sitting in tall prairie grass holding her guitar. I have to remind myself to breathe. She's so beautiful. I automatically save the photo as my desktop wallpaper. Yeah, a bit stalkerish, but nobody gets on my laptop so I'm okay with it. I send Ali a total of three photos. The one of me and Matthew smiling, one of us being silly, and my book cover. I hit send. I don't expect to hear from her for a while. This is the time she naps. I smile because I know her schedule so well already. I'm opening up to her, but I have to remind myself that she's putting a lot of trust in me, too.

CHAPTER ELEVEN

Chalk it up to divine intervention, but Ali and I manage to arrange a dinner date. Her tour bus is passing through St. Louis headed north. That's less than a three-hour drive from camp. I have to convince Ali that I'm fine driving the distance to see her. She's allowing about an hour and a half for dinner. I'm so excited. Our talks lately have been at odd hours, and I'm being patient because I know how frustrated Ali is with her schedule.

After clearing my own schedule with Renee, who wholeheartedly supports this date, I scramble around trying to find something to wear. Most of my clothes are summer casual. Ali's already seen my nice dress, the one I wore a couple of Fridays ago when I had dinner with Tom and Patty. I settle for a semi-fitted yellow dress with thick shoulder straps. It rests right above my knees. It's sexy, but in a subtle way. It shows off my toned body and my summer tan, and makes my hair look even lighter, if that's even possible. Grabbing Renee's keys off the counter, I sneak out before anybody can see or question me. My nerves are on high alert. This is my first date in over a year. The closer I get to St. Louis, the more the butterflies flutter in my stomach. I call up Mr. Frost for the tail end of this journey because I need to calm down and get my mind on something soothing. We dwell on words and the importance of poetry and ways we can revive it. I know that if I try Emily, we will end up talking about death again, and that really isn't going to put me in the best frame of mind for my date. My date. I smile at that and try not to veer off the road in my excitement.

The restaurant we agreed on is on the outskirts of St. Louis. Ali can't deviate too far from the interstate. I'm more than happy to oblige. In fact, I would meet Ali at McDonald's in a different time zone if she wanted. I don't see the tour bus when I arrive. Giving myself one last look over, I head for the door. It takes a few seconds to adjust to the darkness inside the place. It's a sports-themed bar and grill with pennants and trophies and photos of athletes from way back when and the not-so-distant past. It's still quiet and I'm glad. I hate when restaurants are noisy and you have to yell to have a conversation. As I'm explaining to the hostess that I'm meeting a friend, I see Ali sitting in a booth near the back. I'm pretty sure I'm going to melt right there. Ali's look is that of pure hunger, and my stomach flip-flops back and forth. A slow smile spreads across her face as she stands up to greet me. I brush past the hostess and meet Ali beside the booth. I brace for the jolt as I lean into her for a quick, tight hug. Ignoring my lecherous thoughts of her long, firm body pressing into mine, I break the hug and settle into the booth across from her.

"You look wonderful," she says. She reaches out to squeeze my hands. I know I'm turning red from the excitement of seeing her again, not to mention from the heated look she gave me a moment ago. That was a fantastic look.

"So do you. I've missed you." We grin at each other and Ali finally relaxes and leans back in the booth. I can't get over how calm she is. My legs are shaking under the table, and she looks like she doesn't have a care in the world. Here's when

I wish my super power would work. I want to stop time and just look at her. I'm noticing all the familiar things, but I'm also finding different things about her. A tiny scratch on the back of her hand, how her hair is about three inches shorter and parted differently, the tiny freckles on her forehead. She's wearing straight jeans that accentuate her long legs and firm butt. The chocolate-brown V-neck sleeveless shirt shows off her toned arms. Her wavy hair is down, resting right below her breasts, and I'm respectfully trying not to look. Ali's skin is glowing and I have an urge to rub my hand across her arm just to feel her again. I bite my bottom lip and stare at her mouth, remembering our first kiss. I notice Ali's eyes widen in surprise and narrow immediately. I quickly release my bottom lip and ask Ali how she's doing.

"Better now that I'm with you," she says. "Sorry our time is so short. Thank you for coming up and being with me."

"I'm just happy that you're within driving distance," I say. I clench my teeth together to keep them from chattering because I'm jittery and excited to see her again.

"You're nervous," she says. So much for being cool. I respond with a tight smile. "I'm sorry. I shouldn't have pointed it out," she says. "I just meant that it's only me and I wish you weren't."

"Talking to you on the phone is different than seeing you in person." What I really want to tell her is that I find her so incredibly lovely that she takes my breath away and I just want to feel her warm lips on mine again.

"I can leave and call you from another booth." She winks playfully at me.

"No, no. I…I…" I sigh. I don't know how to start or finish the explanation. Without scaring her off, how can I tell her I'm feeling something wonderful again? It's too soon anyway. I'm almost positive she deals with stalkers, and I don't want to be one. She surprises me by sliding out of the booth and standing next to me. I look up at her. She leans down and gently kisses me. It is so soft and sweet, but it leaves me breathless.

"I don't know if that helped you, but it sure as hell helped me," she whispers against my cheek. I don't care that everybody can see us. I can't help but grin, and I'm surprised to find that it helped me. That electricity is still there between us. The same thing I felt when I first saw her. Ali sits back down. I focus on our conversation and try to keep my reactions in check. I fill her in on what's going on at camp, and she tells me about the tour.

"Did you ever help that lady Sara with her website?" she asks.

"Ah, no. I didn't and I don't want to. She's a nice woman, but I have no interest," I say. I hold my hands up, stopping the conversation about Sara Phelps from happening.

"In her or a relationship in general?" Ali asks. I stare at her. Now she looks nervous, and I smile at how quickly things have switched.

"Her no, a relationship yes," I say. I choose my words very carefully. She smiles at me.

"Good," she says.

All too quickly our time comes to an end. As much as I don't want to leave, I know Ali has to get back to her tour.

"Where's the bus?" I ask. I didn't see it when I pulled up.

"It's out back. Everybody's probably napping," Ali says.

I realize our lives are opposite. I'm holed up for months at a time writing, and Ali travels the country for months at a time. Dating a musician is a completely new and different experience. It has to be difficult out on the road away from your home, your bed, your family life. With our differences, I'll have to really think about a relationship with Ali. Am I going to be hurt by a long-term separation? Is the relationship going to be worth it?

"If you need to get going, I understand. I'll see you in two weeks," I say.

Ali smiles at me. "I'm already looking forward to it. Then we won't be so rushed." She grabs the bill, explaining that it's her treat since I drove so far for our date. "No fighting. Come on, I'll walk you to your car. Let's try to get you back to camp before dark."

I lead the way, completely self-conscious with her so close behind me. I can feel her body heat, and I stiffen when she closes the gap even more as we get closer to the door. When Ali touches my elbow to guide me out of the way of somebody entering the bar, I shiver as chills dance across my body. I try to stop it, but I can't. Her touch affects me that much. We exit the building and my spirits sink. I parked in the first spot by the door. Our good-bye will be awkward and in front of everybody at the bar. I turn and offer Ali a ride to her bus. She chuckles and climbs into the passenger seat after helping me into mine. While crawling into the car, my dress rises to mid-thigh. I don't want to draw attention to it by tugging on it so I have no choice but to leave it unattended. Ali has already seen me in a bathing suit, and this covers a hell of a lot more than that. I catch her looking at my legs with a mixture of joy and hunger. Another victory for me. As I drive to the back of the restaurant, my palms start sweating. I know there's going to be a kiss, an awkward hug, or both within the next thirty seconds.

"Thanks again for meeting me," Ali says. Her voice is low and soothing. I smile, reminded why I like hearing her voice. Ali leans forward and runs her thumb down my cheek. My stomach quivers with excitement, anxiety, and possibility. I love this feeling but dread it as well.

"You're welcome." My voice is surprisingly low, too. My eyes lock on Ali's as she leans over and kisses me. Her lips leave mine too soon. I want more and follow Ali back, kissing her fully. I hear her moan and, encouraged, I suck her bottom lip, running my tongue gently along it, feeling the velvety softness, tasting her sweetness. Ali pulls me even closer, and this time I moan. I don't want this to end. Suddenly, I remember that we're in front of the bus and everybody has probably seen us. I reluctantly pull away.

"Mmm. That was nice," Ali says. Her hands are still on my face. I smile weakly, my head and my heart fighting for attention. "Guess I should go, huh?" she says. I nod, knowing both of us need to head out now. "Let me know when you've made it back, okay?" Again, I nod. Why am I not saying anything?

"Be safe." What the hell? Who says that? I mentally smack myself. "Well, have a safe trip, I mean. You know what I mean."

"Oh, I will. And I'll see you in two weeks." She opens the door and steps out into the warm evening. She leans down and winks at me. I wave to her as she climbs the steps of her bus. This is probably the best night I've had. Ever. This is the way it's supposed to feel. The way dating is supposed to be. The warmth, the passion, the want. Smiling, I pull out onto the highway and head back to camp, completely lost in my thoughts of Ali and our incredible evening.

CHAPTER TWELVE

So tell me how you ended up in Chicago," Ali asks me one night on the phone. She's thinking about me because she's headed there for a show. How sweet.

"After Crystal dumped me, I really didn't have a reason to stay in Memphis, so I moved to Chicago. My editor, Tom, is there, and I was always taking trips to see him."

"Did you lose your friends in the breakup?"

"I guess so. I didn't care at that point. Most of them were her friends, and I hated that they knew and nobody said anything to me. I just packed up my stuff and left. I didn't want anything," I say.

"I had the opposite problem. The minute anybody knew a girlfriend cheated on me, they would run to tell me. Sometimes it's better not to know. They had ulterior motives though, I think. Wouldn't it be great to have friends just to have friends?" We both chuckle. "At least tell me you listened to some incredible music in Memphis," she says.

"Oh, most definitely. I've always loved music. I'm sorry I didn't know your music before you showed up at camp. I had a hard time listening to anything that was sweet and romantic. I listen to classical music or straight-up rock. More for background noise."

"Can you listen to me now?" Ali asks softly. I can't tell her that I listen to her every day, every chance I get, and I have several of her songs memorized by now. I can't let her know that I'm giddy when her songs pop up on my iPod while I'm jogging. Sometimes, I have to stop whatever I'm doing because her voice hits something deep inside me and it takes my breath away. I play it off the best I can.

"Of course I can. You have an incredible voice and an incredible mouth—" I stop myself before this conversation turns sexual. I'm not ready for that. "I mean, well, you're simply an amazing artist."

Ali is silent for about five seconds. "Let's go back to the part about my mouth." I swallow hard. She's using the same tone she had when she cornered me at the watering hole right before she kissed me.

"You do have a really nice mouth." My voice is almost a whisper. My mind wanders to the last time I felt her lips on mine. It was when I dropped her off at her tour bus after our dinner. A warm, delicious feeling fills my body, and I can feel my cheeks turning red. I'm clenching the phone and have to force myself to relax.

"What makes it really nice?" she asks.

I think about how her lips are so full that I just want to suck and bite them and how she always says the right things to me and how her voice is so beautiful and clear. I decide not to be so completely raw in my answer.

"They're very delicate." They're like silk against mine, and I almost moan remembering their softness. "Your lips are so red. I don't think I've ever seen lips that red before. And I like watching your mouth when you talk and sing."

"See, now every time I see your mouth, I just want to kiss it," Ali says. I gasp. It's such a simple thing to say, but it sends a jolt through me. How is it possible that this woman, this well-known singer, is interested in a tossed-aside introvert like me? She's not done though. "And every time you bite down on your lower lip, it drives me insane."

"Oh." My mind is screaming things for me to say, but nothing comes out except one tiny insignificant word. "Oh," I say. I repeat it as if I can't believe I said it the first time. Opening up to another person is proving to be difficult. Ali must sense my discomfort because she suddenly changes the subject.

"We're going to have the house to ourselves over the weekend. My aunt and uncle are staying at their condo in town. But they would love to have dinner Sunday night if you're up for it."

"I'd love to meet some of your family." I'm surprised that Ali drops the playfully sexy talk so quickly. I hate myself for not continuing it. I know I'm going to have to open up more with her. I'm ready for this, just scared. I don't know the rules. Yes, I'm definitely attracted to Ali. She's intelligent, beautiful, talented, and flawless. I can't find a flaw. Maybe that's the problem. She's too perfect for me.

"You know what would be nice?" I ask.

"What?"

"We should Skype. I mean, not right now, but sometime. It would be nice to actually see you again," I say.

"I can't believe I haven't thought of that already. Do you have time now?"

Like I'm going to say no to her even though it's one thirty in the morning and I desperately need sleep. I'm so excited. I look down at my clothes and decide I'm okay with what I'm wearing. My hair is a different story. I have it piled high on my head in a messy bun. Sometimes it looks good, but I'd better go check first. I run to the bathroom and give myself a quick check. Thumbs-up.

"Let me fire up my laptop. What's your user name and I'll call you," I tell her. We quickly say good-bye and I type in Ali's user name. Within a few seconds, I see her on the screen. We smile.

"Sorry I'm not dressed for this," she says. She's still in her concert makeup and hair, but she's changed into a tank top. Her long hair is pulled back in a clip. Her cheekbones are high and pronounced, and her strong jaw squares her face. She's too beautiful.

"You look great. I've never seen you in glasses before," Ali says. I crinkle my nose. I forgot I was wearing them. I take them off quickly.

"I only wear them when my eyes get tired from looking at a computer all day."

"No, please keep them on. I really like them," she says. I hesitantly put them back on.

"I get to see you soon," I say, excited. "I know it has to be hard on you out on the road. A few days off for everybody in your band…well, your entire crew, is probably just what everybody needs, huh?"

"Definitely. This is one of my tougher tours and I know we aren't getting enough downtime. We are starting to get pissy with each other and it's just time for a break," she says. She sounds exhausted. "Hey, guess what?" she asks me, her voice softening.

"What?" I'm confused because she suddenly looks serious.

"I'm looking at your mouth right now and guess what I want to do?" she asks.

I lick my bottom lip and scrape my teeth across it, remembering what it was like to feel Ali's soft lips on mine. I totally forget that she can see me like I can see her. A part of me is turned on; a part of me is scared to death. I remember Val telling me it's like riding a bike. I tell myself to relax and have fun with her even though my stomach is in my throat and my heart has floated away somewhere.

"Well, then our weekend is going to be…nice."

Ali's eyes narrow at me. "I'm sure of it." We stare at each other for a few seconds before I break eye contact. I can only be strong for so long.

I ask her about her concert. She gives me a quick rundown and yawns. I can tell she's tired. She stretches and then rubs her collarbone. Her tank top stretches tighter across her breasts. Her nipples are erect and I'm trying so very hard not to stare. I keep swallowing. I actually hunger for her.

"I should probably let you sleep," I say. I'm struck with an incredible urge to touch myself right now. That hasn't happened in forever.

"No, we just logged on. Can we just talk for five more minutes?" she asks.

"Where are you staying tonight?" It's a stupid question, but I need to get my mind off her breasts.

"On the bus. Bob is driving us to Milwaukee. See?" Ali holds up her phone so I can see the inside of the bus. "You haven't been in the bus before, have you?" she asks me. I shake my head. "Well, let me give you the grand tour." She holds up the phone and shows me the tiny kitchen on the left, the bathroom on the right. She walks us quietly past four bunks and I can hear her band snoring. I giggle. She giggles too and walks toward the back. "This…" She pauses in front of a door. "This is my room. I can't sleep back here while Bob is driving, but I spend a lot of time in here before my concerts." She opens the door. I see a full-size bed tucked in the far corner and a ton of storage cabinets on the other side.

"Wow. Nice." I'm surprised at the luxury. "Your bed looks so comfortable." I don't realize the implication until Ali gives me an exaggerated wink. I drop my head into my hands. "Well, you know what I mean. It looks comfortable for a bed on a tour bus." I peep back at her through my fingers. She laughs.

"It's not bad and has really dark shades on the windows so I can sleep," she says.

"You probably get about as much sleep as I do. I'll have to start asking you if you're getting sleep at night instead of you always worrying about me."

"Probably not enough. I get a lot of rest. There isn't much to do on a tour bus except rest, eat, and read. We can't even exercise. I feel like a total lump when I'm done touring. I usually have to do some sort of sugar and fat detox when I'm done," she says.

"How do you do that?"

"I go to a spa in Phoenix for a week. It's the perfect getaway."

"That sounds wonderful. I'm sure you deserve it."

"My mom joins me. And Aunt Judy, the one you'll meet at the lake. It's kind of a new tradition now. Just the three of us," she says.

"That's really sweet. I'm glad you're so tight with your family." I make a mental note to call my mom and check in with her this week.

"How often do you see your parents?"

"Only a few times a year. I know I need to be a better daughter. Maybe after camp I'll head down and hang out for a bit. Texas in August sounds like fun, huh?" I say.

"Well, I envy your small family. It's total chaos with my family over holidays, birthdays, any get-togethers we have. We have to draw names at Christmas because there are so many of us. It's overwhelming. Nice, but just a lot to take in at once," she says.

"And I've always been envious of large families."

"The grass is always greener. I wish we could have a Christmas where one person opens a gift, knows who it's from, says thank you, and we move on to the next person. Half of the time in my family, nobody knows who got what from whom unless it's an inside joke. It loses its meaning at that point. Don't tell my mom, but sometimes I'm purposely a day or two late so that I get to pass out gifts and open them without interference," Ali says.

"You're lucky. I'm usually not around children during holidays. I wish I had that. You get to see your niece's face when you give her gifts. And I know you spoil her."

"Maybe a little bit. My niece is so much fun. Wait until you meet her. You're going to love her. You're good with kids," Ali says.

"How could you know that? I always ran and hid when you showed up."

"Just because you didn't see me doesn't mean I wasn't watching you. And I don't mean that in a stalker kind of way. I just like watching you."

Again, a chill races through me. Her words unbalance me. I'm torn between being completely flattered and justifiably wary. I don't know her dating habits. Historically, musicians are hailed as unfaithful. Not all of them, but I'm sure some are. It would be hard not to fall into bed with people who worship you. Just at the bar that one night, Ali had about eight women surrounding her. Of course she chose me, I remind myself, and smile at that memory. That was the first time we touched.

"I've made you uncomfortable again. I'm sorry. How about we both get some sleep and talk tomorrow?" she asks.

That makes me smile, but I don't want her thinking I'm uncomfortable for the wrong reasons. I know she's not a stalker.

"I think you're very sweet, Ali. It's just going to take some time to get used to you. That's all." I smile and hope she believes me. She winks and wishes me sweet dreams. We hang up. Life is definitely looking up and I'm ready to embrace it.

I crawl into bed still smiling from our talk. I love how she gets me in a good mood. I like the slowness of our relationship. I never understood how people could have sex after one or two dates. What's the connection? I like that Ali is willing to wait with me. I hope I'm worth waiting for.

I think about that moment when I decide to give myself to her and she is able to touch me how she wants to and I can touch her back. I think about her curves and what it would be like to feel her again. I can tell she's going to be the aggressor, and I'm actually excited about it. I've never had a lover take control of me. I think about her kissing me and pinning me down. The idea excites me. I slip my hand down my boxers to touch myself. I'm already wet with need. I rub my slickness up to my clit and gently stroke in tiny circles. Oh, my God, I've missed this. I picture Ali lying between my legs and I slip off my boxers. I know I'm going to come quickly. I slide two fingers inside while still stroking my clit. I wish Ali's mouth was on me. I wish her hands were the ones touching me and her fingers were inside me. I can feel myself climbing higher. I stroke faster and begin moving my hips up and down to find a good rhythm. Within seconds I explode. I lie there for a minute, absorbing the magnitude of this moment. I've actually masturbated because I'm excited about another person. Turns out, I'm fine. I'm better than fine. I'm fantastic.

CHAPTER THIRTEEN

The humidity of an average Kansas City summer night is horrific. I gave up on looking great for Ali the minute I arrived at the outdoor venue. The heat is oppressive. My clothes, what few I'm wearing, are sticking to me. The mist machines really aren't cooling us off, but we're all having such a great time, we don't even care. I'd forgotten how much I love concerts. I smell the heat, spilled beer, hidden weed, and metal of the seats. Separately, not great smells, but thrown together with a beautiful woman singing to us and it's a great concert.

I'm surprised to see young and old people. Everyone is moving to the beat and I'm enthralled. This has a different feeling than the other concerts I've been to. I can feel Ali's heated looks my way when we make eye contact. I know she's singing to me and I couldn't possibly be more turned on. I drag Emily from her Wild Nights and bring her to mine. I'm sure she'll like Ali's music and the atmosphere of a concert from the twenty-first century. Flashing lights, great musicians, and Ali's low, raspy voice singing to the crowd. Not to mention the hundreds of people singing along with her.

"This has been an amazing summer!" Ali yells to the crowd. "I'm on tour, I get to visit the country, and I get to see wonderful people like you." She waits until the crowd quiets down a bit. "And I met someone." The last statement brings the crowd to their feet, and they whistle and holler while Ali stands there grinning. I'm in the front row, grinning, too. She's outed us. Well, technically, nobody knows she's talking about me, but she's made it clear she's now in a relationship. Yeah, me!

The crowd asks her who and several of the concert-goers yell, "me." I feel like I'll burst with excitement knowing we have a secret from everybody else.

"She's here tonight and I have a little surprise for her. Beth, this one's for you." She starts strumming her guitar. I'm sure everybody's staring at me right now even though they really don't know it's me. My heart swells. I'm shaking again. Too many thoughts are racing in my head and in my heart at once. She starts singing and I forget where I am, I forget about the crowd, and I focus solely on her. Her voice is strong, but quiet. I haven't heard this song before, but it's sweet and I love it immediately. It's the best gift anybody's ever given me. I want to run onstage and collapse into Ali when she finishes singing. She bows and says thank you. She winks at me and starts numbering off for her band. They quickly move onto one of Ali's more popular songs, and the crowd goes wild. The woman next to me leans over to yell in my ear.

"She's so great, isn't she?" She's very excited to be here. I am, too. Ali's mesmerizing, and I can understand why people want to be near her.

"Have a great night," Ali yells to the crowd, waving at them. "Thank you for coming out and spending your evening with us!" She puts her guitar down and walks offstage, the rest of the band eventually trailing her after having their fun with the crowd. I feel somebody touch my elbow and look up to see a security guard trying to get my attention.

"Can you come with me?" he asks. He motions for me to follow him. I nod and he escorts me around the stage and up the side steps. I know I'm the envy of every person there, and I'm tempted to turn around and smile. Backstage, I see Ali drinking water and nodding to something her bass player tells her. We make eye contact and she makes a beeline for me.

"So what did you think?" she asks, almost shyly. I don't say a single word. Instead, I lean forward and place a hard kiss on her lips. Ali tastes cold from the water and salty from her sweat. Our kiss softens and deepens and I feel Ali mold herself to me, pushing me into the wall behind us. I hear her moan. My knees wobble. Ali moaning is a delicious sound. She reluctantly pulls away. "I have to go back onstage," she says. She gives me another hard kiss. "Wait right here." I smile at her. She sings two more songs as I stand offstage watching her. I can't remember a time when I was this happy. She struts off the stage and heads for me.

"That was incredible, Ali. I love my song." I give her a tight hug.

"I'm glad you liked it."

Ali's manager, Maureen, reminds Ali that she has a meet-and-greet with her fans. Ali tells Maureen that she'll be there in ten minutes and takes me by the hand, leading me down a long hallway with a lot of rooms. She takes us to her dressing room. I'm not disappointed. It's private, and that's exactly what I want right now.

"That blew me away. Your fans absolutely love you," I say.

"I'm happy I get to do something I love for a living." We sit on the couch and I can feel her energy. She reaches out and pulls me close. We kiss very softly at first. Our passion ignites and I find myself on my back with Ali's weight on top of me. I'm not sure if I pulled her or she pushed me, but either way, I love the feeling of her body completely flush against mine. Her curves press into mine, and I can feel her body heat through our clothes.

"I'm sorry I'm so sweaty," Ali says. She pulls away quickly, leaving me confused. She obviously doesn't know about my obsession with her sweaty body. "We should try this after I get cleaned up." I frown with disappointment and Ali quickly erases it with another kiss. My hands end up under her shirt, touching her hard stomach and sliding downward to her hips. Where did this confidence come from? A knock at the door interrupts us.

"C'mon, kitten, we gotta go," Brian, Ali's drummer, yells. "We're being summoned by the Mighty Mo." Has it been ten minutes already? Ali stops kissing me and sighs.

"All right," she yells back. "Give me a minute." She looks at me with regret. "I have to do this. Do you want to wait here for me and I can get you after the meet-and-greet? We can all go get something to eat."

"I'm kind of tired from driving all day. Can I just meet you at the hotel?" I hope that I sound nonchalant. I want time to clean up before Ali gets there. I'm not sure what's in store for us tonight, but judging from the last ten minutes of our relationship, I'm pretty sure we're going to have sex. I now understand why musicians have a ton of sex. The rushing adrenaline, the screaming fans. It's such an exciting feeling. I get it now. Hell, I want it, too, and I'm just a fan.

"I'll be there as quickly as I can." Ali says good-bye to me and is greeted by Brian as soon as she opens the door.

"Remember, the sooner we do this, the sooner you can get back to her," he says. She hits him in the shoulder and sends me an apologetic smile before the door closes. I release a sigh of longing. Waiting is nice, but I'm done being nice. I want the feel of Ali's skin against mine, want to hear her moan with pleasure at my touch. I want to lose myself in her. I snap out of my daydream and head back to my car. It's been a great night and it's only going to get better.

CHAPTER FOURTEEN

The hotel suite has separate bedrooms with a sitting area nestled in between. I pick the undisturbed room, thankful that I have an option. I'm not sure if I'm ready to go all out and throw myself at Ali. Well, I'm ready. I just don't want to embarrass myself. It's been so long, I'm sure I'm going to fumble around like an idiot.

I drop my suitcase on the bed and check out the view. It's beautiful here. Kansas City is lit up like a Christmas tree even though it's July. It's after midnight and I'm surprised by how tired I am. I was tense on the drive up and nervous and excited during the concert. Now that I'm here and I'm starting to relax a bit, I wonder what Ali will be expecting tonight. I wanted to jump her bones after the concert, but now that I've mellowed, I'm worried. I'm afraid of breaking down in front of Ali. Three years is a long time to go without touching another person. Now, I'm struggling to get back to that place. Part of me is afraid that it will happen again—the loss, the struggle to get up each day—but being with Ali has been so wonderful and I want that closeness. Something blossoms inside me whenever I think of her. I know it's time to let go of the past and embrace my future. I know it's time to move on.

I dig through my bag to find my pajamas and toiletries. I need a shower. I feel sticky and want to wash off the entire day. My shower lasts about twenty-five minutes. Thankfully, I had enough sense to visit a spa before the concert. I have cute toes, cute nails, and I'm smooth everywhere thanks to Nina, a woman I hope to never meet again because I don't think I'll be able to look her in the eye after the grooming she did to my lower half. I put on a pink tank top and pink-and-white boy shorts. What I'm wearing isn't super sexy, but it's cute, and that's my goal. I don't want to be obvious. It's late, and I'm not sure what time Ali will be done with whatever musicians do after concerts.

❖

The room is bright and I jerk awake, confused. For a second, I forget where I am. My memory catches up to me and I look at the clock. It's seven thirty. I jump out of bed wondering what happened last night. I remember showering and crawling into bed, but I have no recollection of any conversation or interaction with Ali other than at the concert. I head toward the bathroom instead of the sitting area in search of Ali. I brush my teeth and fix my hair. I splash cold water on my face and take a few more seconds to survey myself. My shorts are rather short, but at least my ass is safely tucked inside. I throw on a T-shirt and open the door.

The sitting area is quiet and unoccupied. Ali is probably still sleeping. I can't resist. I tiptoe to the other bedroom. The door is slightly ajar and that's just a sign for me to peek in. Ali is curled up on her side hugging a pillow tightly. Waves of her long, brown hair fan out beside her. She looks so peaceful and young, and I have an overwhelming desire to curl up behind her and pull her close. Instead, I quietly step out and head back to my room. I need to be quiet. I grab my laptop and crawl back into my bed, thinking I can write until Ali wakes up. My senses are on full alert so falling back to sleep isn't an option. I'm very much aware of how close Ali is to me, and I'm too excited to relax. After twenty minutes of accomplishing absolutely nothing, I decide to head to the gym to burn off my energy. I change clothes and quietly leave the room.

The gym is quiet and exactly what I need. I work out for an hour and a half, hoping that's enough time for Ali to sleep in. It's almost ten and I'm getting hungry. I slide the key into the lock, and, when I open the door, I see Ali sitting on the couch drinking coffee. Her eyes are bright and welcoming. She gives me such a genuine smile that I actually ache.

"Good morning. I figured you were working out," Ali says. "I ordered room service for us. I hope that's okay."

"That's perfect because I'm starving. Do I have time for a quick shower?"

"Sure, take your time."

I give Ali a quick I'll-be-right-back wave and, with lightning speed, take a shower and dress. I'll worry about my hair and makeup later. When I emerge, I head straight for her.

"I'm sorry I fell asleep last night," I say. She smiles and kisses my cheek softly. I hold my breath, surprised by the gentleness.

"It's all right. You were tired. And I remember someone telling me that if I ever find you sleeping, I'm to retreat quietly. Can I get you a cup of coffee?"

"Please. That'd be great." Room service had showed up while I was in the shower and delivered a breakfast of croissants, jellies, fruits, and oatmeal. On cue, my stomach grumbles and Ali laughs.

"Let's get you fed. I called for a noon checkout. That'll give us time to eat and get packed," she says.

"Thanks again for inviting me. I'm looking forward to

hanging out at the lake and going swimming. Just relaxing with you."

"I remember the last time we went swimming," Ali says, her eyebrow lifting ever so slightly. I knock over the butter knife and it clatters against the plate. I look at Ali and feel the electricity between us again.

"I remember, too." I look down at my plate trying to act like it wasn't a big deal when it was life-changing. A simple kiss jarred me back to reality, back to life. I'm thankful Ali took a chance on me and that she's patient and still interested. I know I have to work through a lot, but I'm here and willing to try. Ali definitely has my full, undivided attention this weekend, and our time together will make or break us.

"I think about you all the time," she says. My heart races. "And I think it's endearing that you're so nervous around me." She leans forward and kisses me. She's entirely too gentle with me. I just want to pull her close and crush her against me. I deepen the kiss, cupping her face in my hands, running my thumbs along her jaw. I love kissing her. I love her strength and feeling her excitement. She pulls away from me and I'm confused. "Well, maybe you aren't that nervous around me." She glances at her watch. "As much as I want to stay here and continue kissing you, I don't want to be interrupted, and we only have an hour before checkout. I think you're going to surprise me this weekend." She brushes a piece of hair from my face and tucks it behind my ear. It's such a simple gesture, but intimate, and I'm shaking inside. She needs more than an hour with me to do whatever it is she's going to do, and I'm ecstatic. Why did I fall asleep early last night? Why am I constantly wasting time with Ali?

Ali's phone rings and she leaves my side to answer it. It's her manager. They talk for a while and I busy myself with cleaning up breakfast and packing. She returns to the sitting room with her bags and her guitar. I smile.

"What?" she asks.

"It's just cool that you're a musician," I say. "And a good one." Ali smiles. I grab one of her bags since I only have one, and we leave the room. "I'll get the car if you want to check out." We argued earlier about me paying for half the room, but she wouldn't have any of it. She agrees to meet me out front and I head for the garage.

❖

The drive to the Lake of the Ozarks is easy and uneventful. During the drive, Ali holds my hand several times. It feels so natural. We wind our way down to her aunt and uncle's cabin and I'm trying not to be overly excited, but it's hard. Ali makes me feel so special because her attention is always on me. I'm sure that's mostly due to the newness of us, but I still love it.

We pull up in the driveway and my mouth drops open. The cabin is really a mansion with massively large windows and three stories. I look at Ali, my mouth still agape.

"This isn't a cabin. This is a castle built out of logs!" I say.

Ali laughs. "The logs aren't real. I believe my uncle built it that way so he'd feel better about calling it a cabin instead of a second home," she says. "He's always so worried about what other people think. Well, what the rest of the family thinks. He's an investor and has done very well for himself."

"Yeah. I think so." We unpack the car and Ali unlocks the door. I'm not disappointed with the inside either. The vaulted ceilings and stone fireplaces, plural, are huge, but still manage to give the room a cozy feeling. I fall in love with the "cabin" immediately. It's private and secluded, and I'm excited to spend the next few days up here with Ali. She slips my hand into hers and gives me a tour, saving the upstairs for last. She leads me into a bedroom with a private bathroom. It's decorated in warm cream colors and dark cherry wood furniture. Very classic look.

"This is your room." Ali gently places my bag on the bed. Before I can question her, Ali points to a door. "I'm right across the hall." She smiles at me. I'm relieved she isn't being presumptuous. I'm looking forward to getting close to her this weekend, but I'm glad she's leaving the decision up to me. I don't know if that's a good thing or not because I'm absolutely horrible at making the first move.

CHAPTER FIFTEEN

L et's get you into some dry clothes," Ali says. She steers the boat back onto the dock. It's ninety degrees out even though the sun has already set, but I'm trying hard not to shiver. Falling into a lake going twenty miles an hour is a mood killer. One second, we're laughing and drinking wine, enjoying a night out on the lake, and the next I'm choking on nasty water filled with dirt, algae, and other slimy things. You can't come back gracefully from that.

"I really, really need a shower," I say. I wrinkle my nose in disgust. Before my impromptu swim, I looked and smelled good. My hair was loose and flowing, my clothes and makeup perfect. I was determined to have sex tonight, but now it looks as if I'll have to wait. Again.

We've been dancing around the whole sex thing for the last day and a half, and I'm done waiting. We both know it's there between us. I'm afraid to make the first move, but I know Ali's giving me space. That just means she isn't going to make the first move either. Stalemate. I want to have a tantrum of epic proportions, but then I remember that I'm an adult and good things come to those who wait. Or some crap like that. We dock and Ali helps me out of the boat.

"I'm really sorry I turned the boat so quickly." Her

apology is so sincere it makes me feel guilty for bitching. I wave her off as if this happens to me all the time. I really shouldn't be surprised. I've tripped, stumbled, and now fallen into a lake around her. I should just start wearing a helmet and elbow pads. We walk up to the house and Ali stops me in the kitchen.

"Oh, my God. You're bleeding." She points down to my knee. Yep, that doesn't surprise me either. I'm sure I did that scratching and clawing my way back into the boat. Add knee pads to that list of protective gear.

"I'm fine. Really." I know I sound ridiculous. I'm bleeding and I'm trying to blow it off like this happens to me all the time.

"Stay here and I'll be right back," she says.

Ali quickly heads to the bathroom to gather supplies, leaving me in the kitchen trying to adjust my dress. The weight of the lake water has pulled it down, showing more cleavage than it's designed to. My nipples are hard and very noticeable. I'm not wearing a bra or panties because I was hoping for a serious make-out session, and now I'm regretting that decision.

"Here, jump up on the counter and I'll take a look at your knee." She pats the counter behind me. I hop up and dry off with the towel she hands me. I smile because we're finally eye level with each other. She looks at my knee and begins cleaning it with hydrogen peroxide. She blows on my knee as she washes the cut, minimizing the sting. She's very focused on her task and is completely unaware that I'm staring. She's gorgeous.

"I don't think you need a Band-Aid, but I can get you one if you want," Ali says, looking back at me. I shake my head and lean forward, capturing her lips in a kiss. She deepens the kiss and tries not to bump my leg. I spread my legs so she can move in between them. Within a few seconds, our kiss escalates. Her hands grab my waist, slide down to cup my hips, and pull me to her. If I scoot an inch forward, just an inch, I'll be against her. As if reading my mind, Ali pulls me closer. I gasp, automatically breaking our kiss. Ali's expression is serious, her eyes almost closed. I watch her lips part, swollen with desire. I run my thumb along her bottom lip, the velvety softness almost undetectable by touch. I want to bite it, suck it, run my tongue over it. I'm shaking. Ali feels my reaction, too, and tries to push away.

"No," I say. "Don't move." I pause. "I want this too much." I'm embarrassed by my confession, but time really is our enemy and I know that it's now or never. I smile at Ali and reach up to soothe her frown away. My smile deepens. Ali doesn't know that I'm not wearing anything underneath this dress and her hands are about to find out soon. I run my hands up Ali's shoulders, up her neck, and wind them in her long hair. I kiss her hard, hearing soft, deep moans inside her chest. Her fingers briefly play with the hem of my dress, then slip underneath and grab my thighs. I wrap my legs around her waist, drawing her closer. Her hands move higher and I feel the exact moment she realizes I'm not wearing panties. Her fingertips flutter for a bit, searching.

"Oh, my God," she breathes against my mouth. I can't help but smile. Ali licks her lips and her mouth slashes against mine, all gentleness gone. She slides her hands back down to my thighs and spreads them farther apart. I can feel the heat of her hands and silently beg her to slide her fingers up and touch me, slip inside me, pound against me until I come. I reach up to unbutton her shirt, but then I stop. Shit.

"Ali, Ali, wait." I break our kiss. She looks at me, seeming confused.

"I so don't want to stop, but I need a shower," I say. I know I look and smell like a drowned rat. I pull away from her. She frowns and opens her mouth, then shuts it again. I see the wheels turning and know she's humoring me. She helps me off the counter. I walk around her, touching her waist as I pass. I don't know how I'm able to walk away, but I do and practically sprint to my room to shower. I lean back against the door and catch my breath. This is really, finally happening. I turn on the hot water and rip off my dress, anxious to wash up. I tell myself to calm down. People have sex every day. Ali is probably used to fans throwing themselves at her, offering her whatever she wants, whenever she wants. I remember Ali grabbing my thighs, her fingers so warm against my skin. I gasp at the memory. I'm desperate for her. Last night got away from us with hardly any physical contact, and I'm sure as hell not going to let that happen again. I finish my shower and throw on a pair of silky pajama shorts and a camisole. The look is perfect. Cute and sexy. I step out of my room to find her and pick up where we left off.

CHAPTER SIXTEEN

I hear Ali turn off her shower and I shiver with a mixture of anticipation and fear. Standing by the bay window in her room, I look out at the moonlit lake without really seeing it. I'm far too anxious to see its beauty. My body is still tingling from earlier and I'm on edge. I'm so ready for this next step. I'm sure that if I hadn't fallen into the lake, we would still be in the kitchen; only instead of the countertop, we'd be on the floor. I hear the click of the door, but I don't turn around. I know Ali will come to me and it'll just be a few more seconds before I feel her touch again. Chills race across my arms and shoulders as I feel Ali's body heat right behind me.

"I can always tell when you're near me. My body responds to you before I actually see you," I whisper. She leans down and runs her lips across my bare skin. Her tongue trails up to my neck and I lean back into her, tilting my head to allow her better access.

"You feel so good," Ali says. Her hands slide down to my hips. She pulls me back until our bodies are completely flush. Her kisses become more assertive, and her lips suck against my neck with passion. I moan and reach up to wind my hands deep in her hair, pulling her closer. When her teeth graze my skin, my knees threaten to give out. My body's on fire even though I'm covered in chills. My nipples are painfully erect and my shorts are already drenched. I can feel slickness on my leg and my body swelling with each intimate kiss. I break away from her long enough to turn around.

"Are you sure about this?" she asks. I smile in response and kiss her with as much passion as I can without scaring her. I push her toward the bed, kissing her until we reach the mattress. Ali sits down and pulls me to stand between her legs. She runs her fingertips over my legs and slips them under my shorts, barely touching my upper thighs. I'm torn between pressing into her and taking my time, savoring every touch. I rest my hands on her shoulders. She moves her hands and slides my camisole up. Her lips are on my stomach. I lean into her, running my fingers through her hair, pulling her even closer. Realizing I'm probably suffocating her, I soften my grip. Her hands slide higher until her thumbs brush the underside of my breasts. I'm done waiting. I lean down until her hands completely cup my full breasts. Her thumbs rub my nipples and I groan. I capture Ali's mouth with mine and we tumble back onto the bed. My body is so alive right now. I feel the roughness and smoothness of Ali's hands and whimper with wanting more. I wiggle out of my camisole, the need to feel her skin against mine so strong. I slip my hands under the T-shirt Ali is wearing and marvel at how smooth and hard she is. Her heart beats against my hand. I lean down and place a small, delicate kiss on her navel.

"I've wanted this for so long," I say. "I've wanted to touch you and taste you and just be with you."

"Oh, God, Beth. Me, too, but I didn't want to push you."

She shivers under my touch, so I continue to explore her body. I nudge her shirt up with my nose, finally tasting her skin. I move higher and higher until it's time to either rip off her shirt or beg Ali to sit up so I can take it off. She reads my mind and quickly removes it. She tangles her hands in my hair, pulling me back down on the bed for an intense kiss. I hear moans, but I don't know if they're coming from me or her. I roll on my back, pulling Ali with me so she's nestled between my legs. We both gasp at the contact. Ali breaks our kiss and stares at me.

"You felt that, too," she breathes. I can't find words right now, so I nod and stare at her lips, wondering why they're so far away from mine. I lick my lips and look into her eyes again. She responds by kissing me, the urgency between us getting stronger and stronger. She sucks on my bottom lip, and her teeth scrape it, bite it, soothe the sharpness with her tongue. It's a phenomenal kiss and I'm ready to come right now. I'm torn between plunging into her and slowing down. Her hips start moving against mine. I can hear little moans escape the harder she presses into me.

If we continue like this, we're both going to come. I want to be between her legs, tasting her, feeling the tension leave her body when she does. I don't want it to happen like this. I need to be inside her and feel her warmth and her wetness. I can't get her panties off fast enough. She's perfect. I slide my hands over her hips and down her thighs. I run my fingers gently up and down her slit, feeling the pearly wetness on my fingers. She moans again against my mouth and I know I have to be inside her. I want to be gentle, but I'm not. I thrust my index finger inside her, and I rub her clit with my thumb. I can feel her tremble in my arms and know I should slow down, but she's pushing against my hand. I break our kiss for a moment, forcing her to look at me. When she does, her eyes are almost closed, her lips swollen with passion. She focuses on me and I slide my middle finger inside her.

"Oh, God, Beth!" Her lips find mine again. I move my fingers in and out until all I'm doing is holding them in place as her hips start moving faster, pushing against my hand. I feel her tighten around my fingers. She's close to coming. "Don't stop. You feel incredible. I'm so close." I hold her tight and pump my fingers inside her.

Within moments, she comes. It's a beautiful sight. Her head is thrown back in passion, her body shaking. I'm in complete awe. I've never been with anyone as passionate and giving as Ali. She slows her hips and eventually stills. I can still feel tiny pulsing quivers inside her. I decide I want to stay here forever. "That was incredible, Ali," I say. I brush her hair away from her face. "You're so beautiful."

We kiss again and I know I'm far from being done. I need to taste her. Right now. I bring my fingers up to my mouth. She moans as she watches. She's deliciously tangy, salty and sweet, and I have to have more. Ideally, I'd plant tiny kisses all over her body, but I'm greedy and I don't want to wait. My trail of kisses goes straight down until I'm between her thighs. God, I've missed this. This whole experience, and with Ali, the intensity is tenfold.

"I want to go slow. I want this night to be incredible," I say. True to my word, I work my mouth all over her body, licking, sucking. I gently finger her core, slow at first, then fast, building her up, slowing her down. When I think she's going to finish herself off out of frustration, I reclaim her clit with my mouth and push into her as far as I can. Her legs are spread and they tremble with every lick. Her breathing is short and raspy, punctuated by sensual moans that almost make me come. Her hands weave in my hair and pull me closer. I move everything faster—my hands, my mouth, my tongue—until she crests.

"Yes, Bethany, yes!" Her entire body tightens. She shakes so much as she's coming that I'm worried. "I can't take any more," she says. I smile. I pleased this woman thoroughly.

"You're amazing." She kisses me. I can't help but smile.

Right now, I'm the rock star and it takes all of my efforts not to burst. I'm steady and sure and confident. Resting on one elbow, I trace patterns across Ali's body with my fingertips and watch her slowly settle down.

"You're killing me." Her long fingers grip the sheet. Her body is slick from our intense coupling and I smile with pride. Yep, I still have it in me. I feel her relax and watch her eventually drift off to sleep, reaching out to me, keeping me close.

CHAPTER SEVENTEEN

I'm somewhere between sleep and reality when I feel Ali's warm hands slowly running up and down my body. I stretch out and press back into them, wanting more. "Ah, so you're awake." Her raspy voice ignites my body. She captures my earlobe in her mouth and bites it. I gasp. Her mouth moves down my neck and sucks the back of it, and every part of me stands at attention. She begins massaging my breast, pinching my nipple, then soothing it with her palm. I'm moaning and I don't care that I'm being loud. I want more. I bring my hand up to hers and squeeze harder, trying to ease the ache she's created. She chuckles at my impatience and turns me over so that I'm facing her. Her lips are on mine, her warm, wet tongue deep in my mouth. Her hands pull my arms above my head and her legs spread me apart. I almost come from the roughness and the quickness of it all.

This is so new for me. I'm instantly wet and I lift my hips to meet hers. I want to touch her, but she still has my hands captured. I realize this is what she wants so I submit. She slowly lets my arms go. I grab hold of the slats in the headboard. I feel her smiling as she kisses me. Her kisses have slowed but are deeper now, and it takes all of my concentration to not wrap my hands in her hair and keep her this close to me. I raise my knees and moan again as her wetness rubs up against me. She runs her hand down my side and squeezes my hip before sliding between us. I'm so tense right now.

"Please, Ali, please let me come." I know I'm begging, but it has been a very long time and I'm desperate. Her fingers flutter along my pussy and I whimper and wait for her to slide inside me. She takes her time, playing with my slick opening. When she touches my clit I break the kiss and cry out. I can't help it. I want her to know what she's doing to me, how incredible I feel. The light from the full moon outside isn't very bright, but I can still see her face and the pure desire etched across it. Her eyes are narrow and her lips are full and her long hair rests over one pale shoulder. She's so beautiful, I want to cry. We're both breathing hard, and she puts her face closer to mine, delivers a quick, soft kiss, and pulls back. We make eye contact again, and that's when she quickly slides two fingers inside me and pushes in as deep as they'll go. I arch my back, cry out, and come instantly.

Holy shit. She doesn't stop, though, and my body stays tight and on edge as she plunges in and out. She slows down only to allow me to catch my breath, then starts over. I'm not disappointed in the least. Her mouth moves down to my breasts. She bites my nipple, then soothes the throbbing ache with her tongue. It hurts, but it feels so damn good. I feel her marking my body, making it her own. She slides lower and I rock my hips back and forth, anxious to feel her warm mouth on me. I want her to skip the in-between journey, but she nips and sucks all the way down, and by the time I feel her breath on my thighs, I'm shaking. I'm embarrassed at my neediness, but not enough to stop her.

She growls, licking the wetness from my thigh. I think I whine, but I'm not sure. I squeeze the headboard tighter, keeping my hands busy. I want to grab her head and keep her close to me, but that would just be rude. She smiles at me and dips her head down, spreading me open with her hands. When her mouth finds my clit, my hips try to buck, but she pushes me down. She licks me hard and fast until I almost come again. She slows down and rolls my clit into her mouth, sucking, bringing me close. My hips start moving when she slips two fingers inside me. God, I want this feeling to last. I fall into the climbing feeling right before I crest, right before my body tenses up, and cry out again. It's just as beautiful the second time. I don't even have words right now. I can't even moan. I can barely breathe.

"You're delicious," she whispers. Her fingers trace tiny patterns softly on my stomach. Her head is resting on my thigh and I could die right now I'm so happy and satisfied. A little self-conscious, too, but not enough to ruin this delicate moment. I bury my hand in her hair. It's still damp from her shower. I run my fingers across her scalp and we both just lie there. I don't want this moment to end. I moan because that's about all I can muster. I feel Ali smile on my leg. This is the best night of my life. Ever.

CHAPTER EIGHTEEN

I slip quietly out of bed, careful not to disturb Ali. It's only seven thirty, still early enough for a jog. My body's sore, but it's a good kind of pain, one that reminds me I'm alive and deserve to be happy. Emily reminds me that happiness is a force that can make me do anything, and I believe her. I glance at Ali, still fast asleep, and smile. We fell asleep around four and I can't believe I'm already up. Adrenaline, I'm sure.

I take care to close the front door quietly so as not to wake Ali, then hit the asphalt hard. What is our future going to be like? I kind of want to know what Ali's thinking and what she wants. Yes, I want to be exclusive, but what does that really mean? I lose days when I write, a definite sore spot between me and Crystal. She had a hard time accepting the time I need to write. I can't write eight to five. I write better at night when Crystal needed me. Ego aside, I can understand why she left me. I picked my career first, but so did she. And my ego's back, or maybe that's my ten-year-old self again.

On top of the whole career thing, I live in Chicago and Ali lives in Massachusetts. Our only time together would be a week or two here and there. Being with Ali last night reminded me of how important it is to have the ability to reach out and touch one another whenever we want. Our bodies were touching the entire night, even after sex. I woke up with Ali's arm over my waist and her legs against mine. I smile remembering. I have a few fresh bruises, and I know Ali's pale skin will show new ones, too. Not to mention the hickeys. I feel like a teenager. I have to be careful with what I wear so the marks on my neck and breasts aren't visible. I know I encouraged her. My neck is very sensitive and it just feels so good.

I look at my watch. I want to cook breakfast for Ali and serve it to her in bed. Besides, the sun is already hot and the roads aren't really designed with the jogger in mind. I'm constantly jumping out of the way to accommodate large pickup trucks towing boats. I reach the house and walk around the courtyard to cool down.

"I was worried when I couldn't find you," Ali says. I stare up, shading my eyes from the sun, and find her looking out of the bedroom window. Her hair is dangling down and I think of Rapunzel. She smiles at me and my heart flutters.

"I should have left a note, but I didn't think you'd wake up."

"Oh, I'm not up," she says. "I just wanted to make sure you're okay. You need to get back up here. I miss you."

I bolt up the stairs. I'm covered in sweat so I make a beeline for the bathroom and take a quick, cool shower. I wrap myself in a towel and head back to bed. Ali's half asleep, but she reaches out for me. Without hesitation, I drop my towel and slide into the warm bed, snuggling against her.

"I can't believe you left this warm sanctuary." She starts nuzzling my neck.

"I can't believe I did either." Even though I'm not really tired, I don't want to interrupt more of her sleep so I lie there quietly and enjoy being held. It's such an exciting feeling, being naked with another person. I can't help but respond sexually. "You're so warm," she says. She lazily runs her hands up and down my back. I love being touched. Her touch is so gentle and even though I know it's a comfort touch, not a sexual one, I will my body to behave. I can't help but moan as her hands explore me. I still them and wrap them around my waist, drawing her closer to me, telling her to get some sleep. She mumbles something, but I feel her relax. Her breathing becomes steady and I know she's asleep again. This is the best feeling, this mixture of need, want, and tenderness. I feel hopeful again. Ali feels like home.

CHAPTER NINETEEN

I can feel tension seeping from Ali. I'm not sure why she's in a bad mood, but I can tell that something's off. After spending four incredible days getting to know her physically and emotionally, I'm hell-bent to find out. This is our last night together and I want to go out with a bang. Or five. Ali is sitting on the floor in the front room leaning against the couch, her guitar beside her, both of them very quiet.

"Are you okay?" I ask. I can tell she's been crying. She smiles up at me and quickly wipes away her tears.

"I'll be fine," she says. She offers no explanation. I'm thinking of every horrible scenario in my head, all at once. Her tour bus caught on fire, something's wrong with someone in her family, somebody died, she hurt herself.

"Why are you crying? Did something happen?" If I don't find out the truth, my imagination's going to get the best of me. That's okay when I'm writing, but not in real life.

"I'm just upset. I'm mad because we're leaving tomorrow morning and it just sucks. I'll be back on the road for two months, and God only knows when I'll get to see you again. It's been so nice and peaceful, just the two of us, getting to know each other. You know? Now we have to go back to text messages and late-night phone calls, and it's just going to be hard."

I'm trying not to think about that, too, but it's been weighing on me.

"I'm really going to miss you." The look she gives me is sweet but sad. I smile at her.

"I'll see you before your tour ends. I'm not going to go two months and not see you or touch you." I drop to my knees so we're eye level. "I've waited too long for you. I'm not going flip a switch and turn off everything I'm feeling just because you're traveling."

I realize that I've just opened my heart to her. I think she needs to know that I'm not Gennifer and I do think she's worth the wait. Ali stares at me for a few seconds and then leans forward and kisses me. It's sensuous and slow, and I don't know how I'm going to handle being apart from her for so long. I vow in my head to see her every two or three weeks.

"I'm going to miss this," she whispers against my mouth. "Your beautiful mouth, your touch, the noises you make when we're together. Just knowing that you're close to me."

My heart tumbles around inside me, trying to stabilize. It ends up in my stomach.

"I'm going to miss you, too. You saved me. You know that, right? Thank you for talking to me that Saturday at camp. You woke up a part of me that I didn't think would ever wake again." I know I sound pathetic, but I'm trying to be sincere and truthful. I kiss her again, putting all of my heart into that kiss. I hope she feels my vulnerability and how close I am to tears, too. Our kiss shifts, suddenly becoming more urgent, more passionate. I want to be naked against her right now. I take off my shirt and remove my shorts to reveal the bikini I was wearing the day at my cabin when she changed my life.

I straddle her and slide down so that I'm sitting on her lap, her knees behind me. Her pupils dilate and she's breathing heavier than normal. Our kiss turns passionate immediately.

Her hands run from my waist, up my back, and twist in my hair to bring me closer. I can feel the roughness of her jeans against my sex. The bikini offers very little covering and I rock my hips for more friction. I'm desperate to feel her hands on me. I want her to make me forget that this time tomorrow we'll be apart. She tugs at the strings of my bikini bottoms, trying to take them off. I tilt my hips a bit to allow her to finish untying. I've never wanted my clothes off faster in my life. There is something so incredibly sexy about being completely naked while Ali's still dressed.

"I can't believe you're real," she says. "I'm the luckiest woman in the world. Just look at you. You're perfection."

I'm not sure how to respond. I watch as Ali runs her fingertips over my stomach and up to cup my breast. I close my eyes when I see her mouth close over my nipple. I lean back to allow her more room. She runs her hands up my thighs and slides two fingers inside me. I lift up to give her more access. I'm moving my hips fast and I feel like I'm going to break her hand. I try to stop for fear that I really will hurt her. She keeps thrusting into me and kissing me and we're moving completely in sync. My knees are scraping against the carpet, but I don't care. I need to come. One of her hands is at the back of my neck holding me in place. She alternates her mouth between my lips and my breasts. We're both sweating and moaning, and when I finally come, I shake so hard I collapse.

"Are you okay?" she asks. She's rubbing my back, trying to calm me down. I can't find words. I can only nod and rest my head on her shoulder. If I look at her right now, she'll see how I'm feeling, and it's too soon for either one of us to go there. I count to ten, then look up at her. She looks so worried that I can't help but smile. I run my hand over Ali's cheek and kiss her softly.

"I'm wonderful," I say. "That was so fast and incredible. It just took me by surprise." She smiles back and runs her finger over my bottom lip.

"It took me by surprise, too." She gently kisses me. "You're going to be sore later. Your lip is swollen from me. I'm sorry." I run my tongue over my bottom lip to feel. "Mmm. I love when you do that." She kisses me again.

It feels so good opening up to another person. I'm relaxing and she's holding me, stroking my hair. I suddenly remember that she was the one who needed comforting. "I should probably get off you and dress," I say. I'm feeling guilty and exposed. Ali sits there with a wicked grin.

"I think you should spend the rest of the day wearing nothing. You know, I've touched you, kissed you, stared at you for days, and I can't find a single flaw," she says. I start getting uncomfortable and she holds my face in both of her hands. She's not rough with me, but she certainly makes me look at her. It's sexy. "You're perfect. Get used to me telling you."

I don't know what to say so I nod. I get up and quickly throw my T-shirt and shorts back on. God only knows what happened to my bikini. Both of my knees are raw. "Look at my knees!" I say. Ali's eyes get very, very wide.

"Oh, my God! I'm so sorry."

"Don't worry about it. Weekend wounds. I've been scarred before. Not this way, though," I say. Ali kisses her index finger and gently touches my knees. She's so thoughtful. I look at her and think she's perfect for me. She seems too good to be true.

"Do you want to go into town for a bit?" she asks. "I've held you hostage here the whole time and thought it might be nice to get out for a bit. We can go see John and hang out at the bar for a minute or two."

Escaping for the weekend isn't reality and I know that, but I want to live this fantasy a little while longer. I want to stay here with her and enjoy the last few hours we have together. Again, I'm being selfish, so I relent.

"That sounds like fun."

"We don't have to go until later so there's no rush to get ready. I still stand by my idea of you running around here naked. But I think you'll have a good time at John's. He's the one who gave me my big break." Ali explains how her uncle's best friend, John, let her play at the bar when she visited during the summers in college. She attributes a lot of her success, especially down here, to him. "He's such a super guy and just the sweetest man you'll ever meet."

❖

We decide to go out on the boat and enjoy the lake before we head into town. It's crowded because of the holiday weekend, but we find a quiet spot and drop anchor.

"I'll try not to fall in again," I say. Ali laughs and tosses me a life jacket.

"I'll drive like a granny and not take any sharp turns," she says.

"You can dump me in the lake again as long as we have the same kind of night."

Ali winks at me. I want more from her. I want her to tell me she enjoyed the night, too, but she doesn't say anything. I don't push. I know she enjoyed it, but it's still nice to hear. I want to know what happens now. Instead of asking, I start fixing our dinner plates. Within a few minutes, we are joined by other boaters who are out enjoying the early evening and getting ready to watch the fireworks show. Jesus, I can't get a break. I'm ready to pout because tonight we will have no alone time. This is our last night until God only knows and I'm sharing it with a dozen other people now, and hundreds more in a few hours at the bar. I was hoping for at least a serious make-out session on the boat.

"How about we get out of here before we become trapped?" Ali asks. More and more boats are invading our little alcove, and if we don't leave now, we'll be stuck out here until after the fireworks. I scramble around, securing our picnic, and give her the thumbs up. We say good-bye to our fellow boaters and get the hell out of there. Thankfully, Ali heads straight back to the lake house. Even though she isn't driving fast, I'm still holding on just in case I lose my balance again. I learned my lesson the hard way.

"Do you want to watch the fireworks from the cabin?" she asks. Not unless it's from the bedroom, I think, but keep it to myself. I don't want her to think that I'm in this just for sex, because I'm not.

"Only if you want to." I almost roll my eyes at myself. I hate answers like that. "I'm fine with watching them or just relaxing on the couch. This is your time off, too." Most adults I know only watch fireworks with their kids. I don't want to offend Ali in case she's really into it. She reaches for me as we enter the cabin and kisses me.

"This is our weekend. If you want to just sit around on the couch drinking wine or talking or whatever, then let's do it. I don't care about the fireworks."

"I like that idea so much better," I say. She grabs a bottle of wine from the kitchen and we get comfortable on the couch. We're sitting very close and I love it. She looks so relaxed and refreshed, and I constantly find myself reaching out to touch her or play with her hair. I can't keep my hands off her. How can I possibly have it so bad for her already?

❖

The bar is in full swing by the time we untangle ourselves from one another and head into town. Ali purposely leaves her guitar at the cabin, afraid that if she takes it, she'll get sucked into playing a set. She really just wants to see John, that's it. We're weaving through the bodies packing the place when Ali's suddenly torn from my fingers. A giant of a man wraps her in a bear hug, and she laughs and squeezes him back. He's at least a foot taller than her, weighs three hundred and fifty pounds easily, and really does look like a bear. Ali turns to me and introduces me to Mr. Kodiak Bear, also known as John.

"This is Bethany Lange," she tells him. She offers him no other explanation and I'm disappointed. I was kind of hoping for some sort of label. He grabs me, gentler than with Ali, and hugs me, twirling me away from her.

"It's a good thing I'm married," he says. His voice is a growl, and he makes me giggle with his overt flirting. He sits us at the bar and takes our orders. Ali asks for a sweet tea and I order a glass of wine. He brings us appetizers. We nibble and talk to John, who swings by whenever he isn't summoned to the kitchen or the register.

"Are you going to sing tonight?" he asks Ali. I cringe.

"Not tonight. I'm taking a break. I can't wait until I can sleep for a week." I rub her back to soothe her.

"When do you head back?" he asks.

"Tomorrow. We're only here for the weekend. A much-needed break," she says.

"Well, let me get another photo for the wall, okay? And no is not an option. Plus your beautiful girlfriend's here, and it's a good excuse to get a photo of her, too!" he says. Ali doesn't correct him and I smile.

Several people in the bar are looking our way. It's either because they know who Ali is or they want to know the beautiful woman in the room. I sigh. Tonight is bittersweet. I'm proud and happy to be out with Ali, but sad that it's our last night together. We really should be back at the cabin, enjoying every minute, enjoying every inch of each other. Ali must have heard me sigh because she calls John over and tells him to take the picture so we can be on our way.

❖

The evening is coming to a close and I'm savoring every minute. I hear the clock strike midnight and sigh. I'm stretched out on the couch, my legs over Ali's lap. She's stroking them softly and I'm in heaven.

"So when do you think you'll be able to visit me again?" she asks.

"Camp closes at the end of the month, so I guess anytime after that. It just depends on where you'll be."

She closes her eyes to think. "I can't remember for sure. Probably on the West Coast somewhere. Most of August is up and down the coast, except for a charity event I have back home for two days. I know we end in San Diego over Labor Day weekend. My whole family shows up for the last concert. They've done it every year since I started touring. Well, at least since I've been somewhat successful," Ali says.

I smile because I'm sure it's an incredible time. I want to be there, too, but I'm afraid to ask. Afraid that it's too much of an imposition.

"Do you have a passport?" she asks.

I nod. I've never been without one. My parents introduced me to the world at an early age, and I try to go somewhere new every couple of years. I realize I haven't been anywhere since the big breakup and decide I need to fix that.

"My parents were always taking me on really nice vacations," I say. Being an only child does have its perks.

Plus it helps when your father comes from money. My grandparents were always sending us overseas during holidays and vacations.

"My favorite place is Italy. The culture is rich and old, and the food is fantastic," she says.

I can't make up my mind. I have too many favorites for all different reasons. Austria for skiing, the Bahamas for sunbathing, Alaska and Colorado for hiking. I tell Ali a little bit about my travels and she's impressed.

"When I go overseas in February, it'll be a quick tour, but it'll mainly be in Europe," she says. I frown. She gives me a frustrated look. "See? This is the part of my life I don't like. Here I meet you, this wonderful woman I'm excited about, and in a few months I'm leaving this again. Us." She motions her hand back and forth. "People think musicians are such shits out on the road, but we just can't seem to keep a relationship strong because we're away for long periods of time." She runs her hands through her hair and worry is etched on her face. I reach out and hold her hand.

"I don't know if I buy that. If people care about each other, they have to trust each other. It's not easy, I'm sure, but if you really want it to work, then it will. What happened with you and Gennifer?" I ask.

"That's a long story." She starts talking and then stops. I'm surprised because I've been so wrapped up in my own life getting over Crystal that I didn't think about Ali and what she might be going through. "I was playing in a bar one night back home. She bought me a drink and we stayed up all night talking. She'd never heard my music before and really liked it. This was right when my career was taking off. She started hanging around whenever I played in town."

"You were together for over three years, right?" I ask before realizing my mistake. Ali tilts her head and looks at me. "When you first showed up at camp, I Googled you and read an article that said you and your girlfriend of three years lived in the same town where you grew up."

"And that's why you stayed away from me that week, huh?" she teases.

I groan. "I know, I know. What a complete waste of time." I rest my head back on the couch. "So, why did you two break up?"

"We didn't want the same things. Being on the road so much really put a strain on us and we eventually grew apart. Genn spent her time hanging out with her friends even when I was in town. I didn't mind that she had friends, but it would've been nice to spend time together. We actually went to counseling for about three months. Obviously, that didn't work. I was interested in starting a family, and she didn't feel like she was ready to settle down. I think she was afraid I'd leave her alone with our kids and be on the road for six months out of the year. I can't and I don't blame her. I'm just thankful we figured out that our problems were unfixable before we started a family."

I'm surprised by her confession. This is a lot of information for her to share. I feel sad. Ali is afraid her career isn't geared for a commitment.

"The irony is that I'd already promised myself that once we got pregnant, I was going to take time off. That's why I toured so much and really pushed myself. I was saving up. The house was free and clear, and I had enough in the bank to not work if I didn't want to. When we broke up, I gave Genn the house and moved back in with my parents." She laughs. "It's sad really. Here I am, thirty-three years old and I still live at home."

I smile. I don't think that's bad. Ali is very close to her family.

"I think that's fine," I say.

"Well, I'll need to get my own place by the time you come to visit. Or else I'll have to come up with creative ways to keep you quiet." Ali shoots me a sexy look, causing me to blush and shiver. "I'm not complaining. You know, the first time I saw you, I had wicked thoughts. I thought for sure I was going to teach you a thing or two." I watch her long fingers stroke my skin, their path headed right for the apex of my thighs. "But after this weekend…" she says. Her voice is thick, her meaning clear. I know she's turned on. I love that I'm learning her moods just by her voice. Well, I've only experienced a few of her moods, ninety-nine percent of them good, so my odds of getting it right are pretty high.

"This has been one of my favorite weekends." My heart and stomach flutter as I think about all the times and ways Ali touched me.

"It'll be hard to say good-bye tomorrow," Ali says. I hear the sadness in her voice. "Too bad I'm right in the middle of my tour. You know something? The gods must have known we'd get together because of this nice four-day break. Remind me to send Maureen something nice."

"Remind me to send her something nice, too," I say. I'm trying to get Ali to smile. "Come on, let's go to bed and make the best of this night." I move my legs off her lap and hold my hand out to her. This is going to be a monster of an emotional night, and I hope I have the strength to get through it without breaking down. She pulls me close as we crawl into bed, beginning a slow seduction. She's being very sweet, but I want to grab her and tell her that by now she should realize I'm a sure thing and she doesn't have to be so gentle. I can tell tonight is different. She's touching me longer, almost trying to memorize me. I miss the confident Ali, but tender Ali is also nice.

CHAPTER TWENTY

The alarm jerks us out of bed. We have about an hour to get ready and another four to drive up to the Kansas City International Airport. After a good-morning kiss that threatens to lead to other things, I reluctantly unwrap myself from Ali's embrace and hop into the shower. This weekend has been life-changing for me. Even if this relationship doesn't work out, I'm happy that I've had a breakthrough and have moved past Crystal. I'm trying to be realistic because I know Ali and I have more things against us than for us. We want the same things, but we're still trying each other out and everything is still so new. Hell, I don't even know Ali's favorite color. I hear the door to the shower open and I smile. Ali slides into my arms. After a heated kiss, I separate myself from her, giving her space to get wet.

"Your favorite color is green," I say. Ali massages shampoo into her long hair. I sigh. I can watch her do the most mundane tasks and still find her sexy.

"It's actually purple. I don't wear the color, but I love it," she says. "Why?"

"I wanted to know something simple about you. Part of the whole getting-to-know-you-thing," I say. It's hard to concentrate with Ali's glistening body right in front of me. "I need to leave right now because if I don't, we won't leave in time for you to catch your flight."

She responds by kissing me senseless.

"All I do around you is moan," I say.

"That's not a bad thing, is it?"

"It is when I'm trying to be responsible and get us somewhere on time," I say. I'm trying to look stern but failing miserably. I slide my hands down Ali's body, avoiding bruises that I'm sure are a result of our weekend. "I'm outta here. Hurry up. I'll start breakfast."

I slip out before Ali can protest. I throw on shorts and a shirt and braid my hair. Breakfast will have to be quick. I'm slicing fruit and adding the pieces to vanilla yogurt when Ali enters the kitchen.

"Are you packed?" I ask. I'm suddenly avoiding eye contact. It's going to be hard saying good-bye.

"Yes, I packed most of my stuff last night. Just need to do a quick walk-through and we can hit the road."

I pour two cups of coffee and set one in front of Ali. I divide up breakfast and slide a bowl over to her as well. I stop moving when Ali touches my hand.

"Hey. Are you all right?" she asks.

I look at her and nod. "Back to reality." I sigh. I continue expelling my nervous energy by tidying up the already clean kitchen. I can feel Ali's gaze on me. I probably look crazy right now.

"We'll still talk every night. You have my schedule, so anytime you can get away, visit me. When I'm done, I'll visit you. It's only fair since you've catered to my every whim so far," she says. "Then you can show me Chicago since I've only been there a few times and never got a chance to do anything fun."

It'll be good for both of us because I've lived there for

three years and have never had the chance to do anything fun either.

"I know. I just hate good-byes. I'm sorry I'm so squirrelly right now," I say.

She reaches out and stops my weird trek around the kitchen. "We will make this work, Bethany. I want this and you more than anything," she says. That lifts me up. "The time apart will go fast and then we can be together again. I promise." She kisses me tenderly.

I lick my lips when she pulls away, keeping the taste of her in my mouth a little bit longer. I nod in agreement, not trusting my voice. We eat breakfast in silence. Even though it's coming to an end, this weekend was the best I've ever had.

CHAPTER TWENTY-ONE

It's late on Thursday and I think about how just three days ago, I woke up snuggled in Ali's arms. It seems like a lifetime ago. Camp has been uneventful and I'm back on laundry duty since I missed Monday. I don't mind though. It allows me private time to be alone with my thoughts and whomever I choose to talk to at the moment. Right now, I'm folding clothes and it's just me and Shakespeare discussing love sonnets and how his perspective is so much more eloquent than mine. The language five hundred years ago was powerful and expressive. It has since been slaughtered and abbreviated, and now we barely communicate as a society unless we use acronyms.

My phone rings and I realize it's Ali on FaceTime. "Hi," she says. Her smile fills up the screen. God, I love her mouth.

"Hi," I say. "How was the concert?"

"It was good. I didn't even screw up once." I laugh because for the last two shows, Ali has slipped up on her guitar, and she blames me for her lack of attention. "What are you doing right now?"

"I'm next door, finishing up the laundry. I'm basically done." I scramble around and shut off the lights. I want to get back to the privacy of my own cabin. Not that anybody can hear our conversation, but I just want to be alone with her.

"Are you back in your cabin yet?" she asks. I nod as I shut

the door. "I have an idea," she says, her voice still low and her words slow.

"Okay..." I have no idea what she's thinking, but based on the look she's giving me, it's going to be intense.

"Slip into bed," she says. I give her a confused look and she elaborates. "Get comfortable. I want to tell you a story."

I haven't said no to her yet and I doubt I will. I smile and do what she asks, eager to hear what she's going to tell me. A part of me thinks it will be sexual. Even during sex, her whispers were low. Incomplete thoughts, really. Hot, from what I can remember, but just words. I try to be calm, but I'm nervous in a good way. I slip under the covers.

"Once upon a time," she says, and I laugh until I see her face and realize she's serious. I stop smiling immediately and listen. She starts again. "Once upon a time, there was a beautiful woman named Beth."

I refrain from snorting.

"She worked at a camp during the summers, and one day she fell on her back in front of a visitor named Ali."

Again, I refrain from snorting.

"Ali thought she was the prettiest woman she'd ever seen and made it her mission to get to know her better, but Beth avoided her the entire time," she says. I give her a sad smile and she stops her story. "I'm glad we did get to know each other." She's serious again and I gulp. She can go from fun to intense in the blink of an eye. "The minute I touched you, I knew I wanted more. Our first kiss I wanted to devour you right there in the water."

"I'm just glad you made the first move. I'm so bad at that," I say.

"You've been so open with me, especially since we made love," she says. "I can't tell you how wonderful your honesty is." I'm focusing on the words "making love," because most of the time the sex was so intense and powerfully raw. I've been avoiding the word "love" because we're so new and I'm trying to not make Ali my rebound girl. Not that I think she really means the word, it's just that I'm word-sensitive, and it's not a word I throw around lightly. I'm arguing with myself when I should be paying attention to her.

"Do you know what my favorite part about our weekend was?" she asks.

Yes, I want to know.

"The way you responded to my touch." I want to moan. She continues. "You're so passionate and you taste incredible. My memory of you, of us, gets me through every day."

I'm on fire. Nobody's ever been this candid with me. I have the urge to touch myself while she's talking to me. Her raspy voice is driving me crazy. I miss her. I need her. I crave her. I try to secretly prop up the phone so I can free my hands, but I fail.

"What are you doing?" Ali asks. Apparently, my frustration's evident.

"Um…nothing."

"Really?" she asks, cocking her eyebrow. She knows. "I'll tell you what. Let me change into my pajamas and I'll call you right back. Thirty seconds or less."

That's not going to give me enough time to do what I want to do. I nod and hang up, sorry for the loss and feeling strangely empty. She calls me back within two minutes, and I wonder if two minutes would've been enough time. I suddenly perk up because now I don't have to hold the phone out so we can see one another while we talk. I quietly slip out of my boxers.

"Where were we?" she asks. "Oh, yeah. I was telling you how much I miss your taste." I close my eyes and slowly begin to touch myself. I bite my lip to keep from making any noises that'll give me away. "I love how wet you are when we're together and how you give yourself to me. You're so warm and so tight, and I just wish I was inside you right now, slowly fucking you." My eyes fly open with that. Holy crap! She's never said anything like that to me before. It's so animalistic. I move my fingers faster and harder, focusing on her voice and listening even harder to her words. "I wish you were right here next to me so I could touch you and hold you and bury myself in you. I miss sucking on your neck and feeling your nails on my back and my legs as you get closer and closer to coming."

God, her voice is so low and sexy, and I'm going to explode. I hiss through my clenched teeth and hope I'm not so loud that she hears. She continues her verbal seduction and I come as quietly as I can. I'm pretty sure she knows what I just did because I can hear the smile in her voice as I come down from my sexual high. I'm a mixture of embarrassed and thrilled, and I want to giggle because I've never done this before. There's no way I can return the favor. I would be a complete awkward mess, and I wouldn't know what to say. I swear, when I hear my voice on a recording, I cringe because I sound like Minnie Mouse. I do not have a sexy voice. I can't imagine it turning Ali on enough to masturbate.

"How are you, sweets?" she asks.

Fantastic! Wonderful! Incredible!

My breathing is still ragged and I try to control it. "I'm very good now." I don't tell her what I just did because she already knows, and she's kind enough not to tease me or talk about it.

"I wish I was there right now," she says. She doesn't know how much I wish she was here, too. "You should probably get some sleep. Thank you for an incredible night."

I wish I could kiss her. That's always the best way to top off a delicious orgasm.

CHAPTER TWENTY-TWO

I want to drop to my knees to kiss the tarmac when I step off the plane, but I refrain for fear of being run over by other disgruntled and frightened passengers hot on my heels. That was the worst flight I've ever been on. It was a short night flight to Bradley International Airport in Connecticut, but we flew through turbulent winds almost the entire time. My fingers still ache from grabbing the seat and the guy beside me the entire trip. I kept apologizing to him, but he just laughed like it was no big deal. Of course, he drank the whole flight, and I would have, too, but I need to be sober to drive.

I'm done with Camp Jacomo this year and on my way to surprise Ali near her hometown. She's putting on two shows for a charity event, and even though I told her I wouldn't be able to make it, I moved heaven and earth and here I am. I'm extremely excited to see Ali again. It's been a month since our weekend together. Since then, my entire life has been thinking about Ali, dreaming about her, talking to her, or talking about her. She's passionate, exhilarating, sexy, and has unleashed some pretty intense emotions in me.

I was wary of them at first, but then I realized I deserve happiness. So does Ali. We both have been through some tough breakups. I've been so focused on myself that I haven't really given her the time to heal. Her breakup was less than five months ago. I try not to think that I'm probably her rebound girl because, in my heart, I don't believe that. I'm trying hard not to be clingy, but I'm falling short.

My rental car is waiting for me and I drive off, anxious to get to the concert hall. The flight was delayed and I'm not happy about missing the show. It's eleven thirty, and by the time I find the venue, it'll probably be over. There isn't anything I can do about my tardiness so I let it go. Instead, I focus on Ali and her reaction. She's going to be shocked to see me. I wonder how I'll surprise her. Will I be able to get close enough to her and maybe sneak up behind her? Or should I find Brian and ask him to let me on the bus and I surprise her that way? I scratch that idea because they'll probably go eat somewhere and then drive off with me asleep in Ali's bed.

Parking is almost impossible when I get to the hall, and I don't find a spot for three blocks. Great day to wear heels. I wonder how I'm even going to get in as I check all the doors. When I reach the back, I find a security guard smoking outside. I tell him I was at the concert and I've lost my car keys and I'd really appreciate it if he let me in so I can check around my seat. He lets me in, but not until after he spends about twenty seconds letting his eyes roam over my body, resting not too gentlemanly on my breasts. Ugh. I try not to look repulsed and quickly dart past him. I walk through a maze of hallways until I find what I think are dressing rooms. I knock on a door and hear a muffled welcome. I cautiously open it. Brian's inside, sprawled out on the sofa, drinking a beer and talking on the phone.

"Oh, hey, Beth. How are you?" he says.

"Hi. Good to see you again. I'm looking for Ali. Is she around?"

"She's two doors down. Go on in. I know she'll be excited to see you again." I wave thanks and do everything to not run full speed to Ali's door. I make my way down the hall and stop when I see the door to her dressing room ajar. Ali's propped up against the vanity, her legs stretched out in front of her. What I don't expect to see is another woman leaning against her. Ali has the back of her hand on the woman's neck and they're sharing a tender kiss. I turn cold immediately and my vision goes white. I see nothing but white. I know I haven't passed out because I've turned and am making my way back down the hall.

I've always written people seeing red in extreme fits of shock. I'm going to have to change that.

"Is she not there?" Brian asks. I almost crash into him. I shake my head and continue down the hall, trying to get the hell out of this place. I can't wrap my mind around what I just saw. I can't believe it. How can she do this to me, to the fledgling us? I lock my emotions deep down somewhere. I need to get the fuck out of here.

I hear Brian curse and then a lot of other noise and voices. I finally make my way out of that labyrinth of darkness and burst out a side door. I need air. I gulp it greedily. Ignoring all the people around me, I push my way through the crowd, eventually breaking free. I search for my car. I can't remember what kind it is, so I hit the button until a see flashing lights and hear a honk. I lock myself inside and allow the tears to flow. I cry for so many different reasons. I cry because I trusted Ali and I cry for my breaking heart.

I ignore the buzz of my cell phone, knowing full well it's Ali trying to give me some explanation. Nothing she can tell me will make it acceptable for her to kiss another woman or to think that I'm okay with it. I silence my phone. I'm suddenly very tired, and I rest my forehead on the steering wheel, the tears still flowing. I haven't reached that sobbing point, yet, but that will happen when I'm not in public where people can see and judge me. I'll wait to collapse at whatever hotel I pick. I need to find one soon because I'm exhausted.

Bam! Something loud hits the side of the window. I look up in surprise.

"Open up, Beth." It's Ali and she looks as bad as I do. I shake my head no, thankful that my dad always taught me to lock my door whenever I get into a car. I don't want her near me. I don't want her touching me, and I'm wondering how I'm going to get rid of the feel of her touch.

"Please! You don't understand!" she says.

I don't look at her. I can't look at her. I wipe away my tears. I can't let her see me this weak. I need to escape. I watch her check all of the doors on my car. I even double-hit the lock button, thankful she can't get to me. I'll do something stupid like forgive her. We're starting to draw a crowd. She looks desperate and I'm sure I look desolate. She glances around, and I think she's trying to find something to break my window. This is just too much for me. I start the car. She turns and puts her hands on the hood.

"Don't do this, Beth. We need to talk."

I turn up the radio so I can't hear her. She smacks her palms on the hood, and I back up and move into traffic, not really caring if I bump into any cars. Thankfully, I don't. I turn the wheel and keep my eyes in front of me, trying desperately to not look at Ali. Out of the corner of my eye I see her slide down the wall and put her head in her hands. I want to go to her, but I can't. My ego won't allow it. My heart won't allow it either.

I drive slowly, knowing that I'm not in any shape to be on the road. I don't even know where I am so it really doesn't matter. I remember the general direction of the airport so I head toward it. My hands are shaking, but I grit my teeth and push through the heartache. I need to find a room soon. I'm about to fall apart into a million pieces. I see a Hampton Inn and turn the car that way. Somehow, I make it to the parking lot and head inside. I know I look a mess. I get a room and grab my bag from the car. I barely make it before I crumple to the floor. Thank God hotel doors close automatically.

I really don't know how long I'm on the floor before shame picks me up and I head for the bed. I want to just lose myself in sleep, but my thoughts are too painful. My logical side tries to reason with the emotional side. We physically had one day, one dinner, and one long weekend together. We never talked about a committed relationship. Ali asked me if I was ready for one, but we never solidified us. We Skyped or talked on the phone every night, and I really can't believe Ali had the stamina to perform, talk to me every night, and sleep around with other women on the road. I don't want to believe that I invested so much of myself into what I thought was a blossoming relationship only to find out it was just about sex. I'm so exhausted. I know I shouldn't turn my phone on, but I convince myself it's for safety. I find fourteen missed calls from Ali and several texts.

Where did you go? It's not what you think. Please come back.

Please talk to me, Beth.

I need to see you. Call me.

Now, I'm angry. Nothing she can tell me makes it okay for her to kiss another woman. I won't take her call, but I'm not just going to let this stew.

I can't believe you! I trusted you! With everything. All of me. You broke my heart, Ali. I'm done talking. Forget this. Forget us.

I realize I'm crying as I type my message back to her. I don't want to be done with her, but once a cheater, always a cheater. I hit send, wait a minute until I know it's gone through, and turn my phone off. Now, I can try to sleep. That is, after I push everybody out of my head. I don't want to hear Shakespeare tell me that the course of love isn't smooth or Emily preach to me that I should keep my heart open. I want to deal with this the way everybody who's had a broken heart has dealt with pain. I want to wallow in self-pity and pout and cry and analyze every word spoken to see if I read too much into it. I need to cry the rest of these tears, wake up tomorrow, and figure out a way to erase the last two months of my life.

CHAPTER TWENTY-THREE

I stare out the window and watch the people below scurry along the sidewalks and streets of my city. They remind me of marching ants all moving in single file. I feel distant from them. I now understand Emily and the funeral in her brain she's been telling everybody about for years. Hell, I'm there, serving food and waiting on people at my own heart's wake. I can tell I'm depressed. I've been home two weeks now, and I've only had conversations with Tom.

He keeps telling me we aren't on any deadlines and it's okay if I need to take a break. I'm ignoring him. My fourth murder-mystery book was easy to finish because it didn't allow me to think of anything other than the storyline. The other book, the one Tom's been gently pushing me to finish, is the real culprit. I'm trying to distance myself from it, but it keeps dragging me under, stirring up emotions I don't want to have. A week ago, when I dropped by the office, Tom casually mentioned that Ali had reached out to him.

"I really like where this book is going. I think you need to get the anger out and try to start healing. Oh, and Ali Hart called me trying to get in touch with you. Be sure to watch your word tenses. And eat something." That's not verbatim, but damn close. I perked up a bit when he mentioned Ali's name, but my anger kept me in check. I pretended I didn't hear that part. He watched me closely and I stared back at him coolly. He raised his eyebrows and wisely moved on to a different topic. I left there feeling numb, but not beaten.

I know I'm going to have to reconnect with the outside world soon. I haven't read any emails from my main email account. My parents need to know I'm okay because I still haven't turned on my phone. I'm tempted to get a new one, but I don't want to go out. I want to stay in my cocoon of misery, also known as my condo. Tom knows I can hole up for weeks. He and my parents both know what I'm like when I'm close to finishing a book. They respect me and leave me alone. My parents because they know I have a quiet and dark side, and Tom because I'm making him money. That's not fair, because he does care about me, but he has a dozen different writers and I can't monopolize all of his time with my emotional breakdowns.

I make myself a cup of hot tea even though it's a sweaty ninety degrees outside. I circle my laptop. It's time to get back to reality. Too many things are happening right now. I turn on my laptop, and the first thing I see is Ali with her guitar. Sucker punch. I'd forgotten that she was my wallpaper. I've been writing on my netbook this entire time. I want to close my laptop and crawl back into bed, but I can't keep wallowing. I look at her face and smile sadly. I do miss her. I know I was probably unfair with her, but damn, it hurt! It seems like a lifetime ago. At least now I'm calmer than I was a few weeks ago. The intensity of my jealousy scared me. I was a complete wreck and out of control. Yes, I know I should have at least listened to Ali, but I knew I wasn't going to be fair to her or to myself with both of our emotions raging.

I click on my email and cringe. I have over two thousand messages in my inbox. My eyes flicker over the senders, consciously looking for Ali's name, even though I don't want to admit it to myself. I have twenty-four emails from her. I ignore them and weed through the rest. I answer a few from Renee and Val. Apparently, Ali reached out to Renee, too, trying to reach me. I'm thankful nobody gave Ali my home address. If and when I let her on my turf, it will be on my terms. I also ignore the nagging disappointment that nobody gave her my address. I can't win this internal struggle. After two hours of deleting and answering messages, I'm down to only Ali's. Am I ready for this? Am I calm enough to respond? Curiosity wins and I click on the first one, written the night of the concert. I read the words carefully and I'm transported back to that night. I can't forget Ali's hand on that woman. I find out she's Ali's ex-girlfriend, Gennifer. I can't forget their lips touching. My heart hurts again. The ache deep inside almost takes my breath away. I reread the words until they sink in. Until they push through the darkness and anger and I'm able to concentrate on their meaning.

> *Beth,*
>
> *You have to believe me that nothing happened between me and Gennifer. She showed up at the concert to let me know that our dog died. Yes, she wanted to try again, but I said no. I told her I was very happy with somebody else. This sounds really stupid and it really was stupid, but the kiss you saw was a good-bye kiss. It was very chaste. There was no passion. Not what you and I share. When Brian told me you were here, I was so excited, and then he pointed out what you saw and I was a complete wreck. I still am. Please talk to me. Please call me. I need you.*
>
> *Ali*

I received two more emails that night. It's obvious that Ali didn't sleep at all. The explanation seems plausible, really, but it still was hurtful to see. I read the next few. They all have the same message asking me to call her or text. Eventually, the pleading stops and the emails are more informative of the tour and less personal. The very last email she sent me two days ago stops my heart.

> *Bethany,*
>
> *If I knew where you live and if I didn't have a lot of people counting on me to finish this tour, I'd bang down every door in Chicago trying to find you. It's apparent you don't want to talk to me, and as heartbreaking as that is, I have to respect your decision. I just want to make sure you're okay. I can't change what happened. I made a mistake. I hurt you after you gave yourself to me, and I can't forgive myself. I won't try contacting you anymore, but I need to make sure that you're safe. Please at least let me know that. For what it's worth, our time together was incredible and you'll always be in my heart. Please take care of yourself and know that you've changed my life for the better. I wish you true happiness and deserving love. Always.*
>
> *Ali*

I close my eyes and relive our very last kiss. I was dropping her off at Kansas City International Airport, both of us trying hard not to cry. Our kiss was very passionate. It was also in front of everybody at the airport. We hugged for a good minute, neither one of us wanting to let the other go. Eventually, I peeled myself from her embrace and tried smiling. We were both sad though.

If I'm completely honest, I know that the kiss Ali shared with Gennifer was nothing but what Ali said it was. A good-bye. I know that Ali cares for me, and besides, it's not as if we were exclusive or talked about being monogamous. I know that I'm being unfair and I need to talk to her. It's the right thing to do.

Ali,

I'm fine. I really don't know what to think or say. I know it wasn't very responsible of me to just disappear, but you hurt me. God, it hurt to see you with your arms around somebody else. I know we didn't have an agreement about our relationship, but after our weekend, I assumed we were exclusive. That was my fault. I shouldn't have fallen so hard for you so fast. I get that now. Maybe when I settle down and finish my writing and you're done with your tour, we can meet somewhere and talk. I just can't right now. I don't have the energy or emotional strength. I'm focused on wrapping things up with my book, and I'm so close to finishing it that I owe it to myself to see it through. Please understand that. Good luck with the rest of your tour.

Bethany

I know that my email to Ali isn't much, but it's something. It has hope. A part of me wants to run back to Ali because I miss our closeness. I ache for her touch, and I'm almost ready to forgive her without actually talking to her first. I mentally smack myself. I deserve respect. Being vulnerable is one thing, but allowing somebody to hurt me is just stupid. I've had enough hurt for one lifetime. If I'm going to have a future with Ali, we're going to have to set guidelines on acceptable behavior while we're apart from one another. Kissing other women will not be on my list anywhere.

My computer chimes. I'm surprised that Ali has replied.

Thank you.
Ali

That's all it says. I frown. I want more. I'm greedy for more. Yes, I know I'm being ridiculous and selfish, but thank you is a total letdown. Of course, in all fairness, my response to Ali was borderline clinical. I sigh and log out of my computer. I grab my netbook and open the manuscript. I want a fairy-tale ending for this book, but reality isn't going to oblige. At least not yet. The chapter I'm working on now focuses on hope. That's the word of the day. I do have hope for us, but it's more of a seed than a blossom. Baby steps, I convince myself. I tackle the issue of trust and hope and how both are necessary to move forward and how it won't be easy. Not for me and not for a lot of other broken-hearted people.

CHAPTER TWENTY-FOUR

I have to tell you, Beth, this is the best writing I've seen from you. I didn't think I was going to appreciate it as much as I did," Tom says. I nod along with him, cracking a smile that feels foreign.

"It wasn't easy and it's not what people expect from me, but it really helped me move on. I can talk about Crystal without getting upset. It helped me heal. You'd think that by bringing all of this back up, I'd be a wreck, but I'm doing okay. I needed to do this," I say.

"Well, it appeals to your present fans and will hopefully help people who don't know how to deal with break-ups. It's fantastic. It's sad, funny, emotional, and, when I finished it, I wanted more. I need to know more about what's going on and what your next move is," he says.

"I don't even know my next move. I really wish I knew how this is going to work out." I sigh.

"I'm sure things will turn out fine. Just have a little faith."

My smile feels better this time. "You're sweet. I guess I need to talk with Ali and see what comes next."

"Make sure to take some time for yourself. Go celebrate. Go to the park and get tan lines. I'll submit this to Kyle, and once we get his giant stamp of approval, Patty and I'll take you out to a fantastic dinner. Who knows? Maybe by then we'll get to meet this Ali girl."

I hug him and leave his office. The giant weight that was on my shoulders is gone. I feel free. I stop by my place and change into running clothes. I haven't spent any time in Grant Park and I miss my daily runs. Since it's midday Monday, not too many people are around. I feel invigorated out in the sun. I feel new. It's time to start making big-girl decisions. Now that my books are done, I can focus on my future, mainly Ali. I haven't received any more email from her, and as much as that stings, I understand. Her final concert is Friday night in San Diego. Ali's family always attends that one. If I count all of her family members, twenty people will be there, not to mention the band and their families.

I finish my jog and sprawl out on the soft grass, my arm serving as a pillow as I stare up at the sky. I close my eyes and simply enjoy the warmth and listen to the sounds around me. An older lady and her dog are close by playing ball, birds are chirping all around me, and I can hear a group of kids kicking a soccer ball around. I know I'm going to fall asleep. Not a safe decision, but I'm emotionally exhausted. I end up sleeping for an hour. I wake up feeling surprisingly refreshed and walk home, ready to plan the rest of my week.

CHAPTER TWENTY-FIVE

I'm pacing around my phone, staring at it and avoiding it at the same time. Today is the day I'm going to call Ali. Of course, I said that yesterday, too, but today I believe it. I've been debating whether I should call her now or wait until the tour is over. Since I'm done with both manuscripts, I have nothing to do except think of her. God, I'm so nervous. The phone feels like a brick. I automatically find her in my address book. I stare at the thumbnail attached to her number. I've missed her face. I take a deep breath and hit call before panic sets in. I put the phone up to my ear and wait.

"Beth." Her voice is low and raspy. It hits me with such force I have to sit down.

"Hi," I say, not sure how to start the conversation without sounding weird. "Is this a bad time to talk?"

"No. How are you?" She sounds tired. I'm sure the last half of the tour was stressful.

"I'm all right." I'm not going to start in with how I'm not sleeping and my days are hell without her or how my clothes don't fit me anymore. I need to find out where we stand before I fall apart. "How are you? Only a few more days on tour, right?" I pretend like I don't know, but I know her schedule forward and backward. Her last concert is this Friday, only three days away.

"I'm okay. I just can't wait until I'm done with everything."
She sounds defeated. "Thank you for calling. It's so good to
hear your voice."

It's my turn to speak, and I'm torn with how I want to
approach getting together for a talk. The phone seems so
impersonal and I want to see her, but I'm nervous. Maybe too
much time has passed and she's moved on. Maybe she's just
not interested anymore. I did push her away and hard.

"Maybe this isn't the best time to talk, but I would like
to see you," I say. She's quiet for what seems like hours but is
really only about two seconds. Still, I'm nervous.

"Please," she says.

That's exactly what I want to hear. Her voice is sure and
strong, and I know she wants this, too.

"When is a good time?" I'd like to see her in concert
one last time before her tour is done, but I don't want to be a
distraction.

"Is today too soon?" That makes me smile. "If you can
come out to California this week, that would be wonderful. I'd
love to share my final night with you."

"Won't your family be at your concert? I don't want to get
in the way of your time with them."

"Trust me, you're not an imposition. They'll be busy
doing touristy things anyway. I just have to take my niece to
the zoo Friday morning."

"Without the rest of the family?"

"I promised her last week. She was upset because I
haven't been around. My sister put her on the phone with me
and voilà! I have a date at nine a.m. with a four-year-old," she
says. "Hannah made it perfectly clear that the rest of the family
wasn't invited, and I'm totally cool with that. But that's really
all I have to do. If you can make it to the concert, that'd be

great. You could hang out backstage. Or I can fly to Chicago and we can meet over the weekend."

"I can come out there. Let me check into flights and figure something out, and I'll email or text you." I know that sounds so remote, but I have to approach this carefully.

"If you've ever wanted to go to a fantastic zoo, then Hannah and I'd love to escort you on Friday," she says. She sounds hopeful and I so want to jump back in with her, but we have to talk about so much. I just can't go running back as if nothing happened.

"I'll have to check. I have to tie up some loose ends here before I can do anything." I'm lying. I'm so ready to get out of here.

"Did you finish your manuscripts?" she asks.

"I did." I'm proud and sad at the same time. Elated that I'm done, but it's always sad to say good-bye to my characters. I was happy finishing my heartbreak book, but not with the ending. I wanted a quicker, more cheerful finale.

"I'm happy for you, Beth. Really." I hear a commotion and she muffles the phone for a few seconds. She comes back to me and sounds down. "I'm sorry, but I have to go. Will you call me later and let me know what you decide?"

I agree. I'm very surprised at how calm I've been during our conversation. Of course, it's over the phone, and I'm sure it'll be a very different story face-to-face.

"Thank you for calling me. It's so good to hear from you," she says. Oh, how I've missed her low voice. I can hear people behind her talking and know she needs to go.

"See you soon." I hang up, put the phone down, and take a deep breath. I did it. I don't know that I'm ready to meet her family before we actually talk things through though. That could be awkward. I fire up the laptop and look at flights. I decide to catch an early direct one Friday morning, which should put me in about noon. Maybe we can talk that afternoon. I look for rooms at her hotel, but it's booked and I breathe a sigh of relief. I might be tempted to give in to her if we're at the same hotel. The Westin across the street has rooms and I grab a suite there. I deserve it. I don't indulge myself often, but this is a big deal and why the hell not? I wait a few hours to text Ali with my information because I don't want to look desperate.

Chapter Twenty-six

I'm standing at Ali's hotel door, my whole body quivering. I've prayed all day that I remain strong and don't break down the minute I see her. I stare at the numbers on the door for entirely too long. Mr. Frost is right here with me encouraging me to knock. I never take chances. I tell him this is all new to me and he only smiles. I want to roll my eyes because he's a man and simply doesn't understand my anguish, but deep down I know he's right. I'm about ready to knock when the door suddenly opens. Ali looks at me in complete surprise. We stand there a few seconds, neither of us speaking, simply looking at each other. Okay, she's looking and I'm visually devouring her.

"Hi. I was just going to leave the door open for you," she says. She steps back for me to enter. She's sort of whispering and I wonder what's going on. "Please, come in."

I bravely walk by her and can hear her humming. She looks tired, excited, and beautiful. She's dressed casually and her hair's down. I want to wrap my hands in it. I think about that a lot around her.

"Hannah's asleep on the bed." She points to the other room where I see a small form in Ali's bed.

"How was the trip to the zoo?" I turn to face her. I can feel her heat and smell her sweetness, and I take a tiny step back. I'm not ready for her to be so close to me. She must see this because she steps back, too. She doesn't answer me but stares at my face. She looks into my eyes, then drops down to look at my lips and my entire face as though she's trying to memorize me.

"I can't believe you're here," she says. She hasn't moved and I can't really get around her without touching her so I just stand there. Her hands are planted firmly on her hips, and I'm trying to figure out which Ali is in front of me. Because she hasn't taken a step toward me, I'm ruling out confident and tender. I think this is her, vulnerable, waiting for me to make the first move.

"Do you want to talk now or do you need to rest?" I ask. That sounds stupid, but I really don't know what to say. She's so close and I'm completely off-balance. Eye contact is hard, but I need to stay grounded so I make myself look at her.

"Now is perfect. Let's have a seat." She points to the two couches in the other half of the hotel room. She sits down and allows me to sit where I'll be comfortable. I choose a spot close enough to her to have a quiet conversation, but far enough away that I can't reach out to her if and when I become weak. Seeing her, I want to kick my own ass for being jealous and stupid and wasting a month. She's leaning forward with her elbows on her knees. We both start talking at the same time.

"Beth, I want—"

"I think we—"

We both smile.

"Let me start, please," she says. I'm okay with that. "I've been miserable the last month. I don't mean depressed, I mean miserable. I was a dumbass for allowing Gennifer in my dressing room. I should have never, never done that." I can tell she's getting angry at herself all over again, and as much as I want to lean forward and place my hand on her knee to calm her, I don't. She needs to get this out and I need to hear it, regardless of how much it hurts. "I wasn't expecting her, but she convinced Maureen that she had something important to tell me and Mo let her through. Nobody in the band is allowed to let anybody see me anymore unless it's family or you."

Ali relaxes a bit and leans back on the couch. She rubs her hands over her face. When she turns back to me, I see tears gathering in her eyes. Oh, God. I can't. I'll be a sobbing mess right beside her if the tears fall.

"I hate this, Beth. I hate being apart. I miss you so much." Her voice hitches and I know she's fighting the tears. "I swear to you, nothing happened with Genn. You're everything to me. I would never jeopardize us." She rubs her face before she continues.

"We kissed, but it wasn't a real kiss. I know that doesn't make sense, but it really wasn't. I told you why she came to see me. Yes, she was interested in getting together, but I have zero interest in her or a relationship with her, including friendship. The kiss was truly a good-bye." She pauses to slow herself down. "I'm not that kind of person. I'd never lead you on and then do something stupid like cheat on you." She turns to me and this time I see anger in her eyes. "The minute we kissed at camp, I was committed to you. At least in my head. Premature? Probably, but you're what I want. You're perfect. You're beautiful, smart, funny, shy, and sexy. I've never been so taken with anybody before in my life." She looks at me expectantly.

I have no idea what to say. Surprisingly, I'm still here in the conversation. Nobody has mentally whisked me away. Oh, they're all here waiting anxiously, but not a peep from them. This is now my decision. I take a deep breath.

"I know that you know you hurt me so I'm not going to

go on about that. I've hated this past month. I know we never agreed on a status for us." I use air quotes around the word status. "I need that though."

"I want that, too," she says. "Sorry for interrupting. Tell me what you expect. Tell me what you want, what would make you happy."

I'm hoping she already knows that, but I tell her because if this is going to work, she needs to hear it from me so there isn't any doubt.

"I don't feel comfortable with your hands on other women and definitely don't want you to kiss them." I quiet my voice when I realize Hannah's still asleep in the other room. "I want somebody to be faithful and miss me when they're away from me. I want somebody to think about me all the time and wish I was with them. It's normal relationship stuff. If I don't have that, it's just not worth it." As the words are coming out of my mouth, I realize that's what I do have, well, did have with her. I sigh. I know I was extremely upset and jealous, and I overreacted. "Do you think we can get there?"

Ali reaches out to me, then pulls back.

"I know we can, but you can't shut me out every time you get upset. We have to talk about things. We wasted an entire month because you didn't want to hear anything I had to say. That's not fair to me or us," she says.

"It was wrong for me to shut you out, but I needed time. My last breakup put me in a bad place. You know that. Yes, I screwed up by pushing you away, but I'm here now, right?" Now I'm getting worked up again. I don't want to ask, but I have to. "Has there been anybody else? I mean, since me?" I feel like a complete jackass, but I can't help it. Her answer will determine where we pick up and if we pick up. She shoots me a look that I've never seen before, and anger flashes in her eyes.

"Are you really asking me that? After everything I just said to you? After everything I did to reach out to you? Give me some credit here." She's definitely angry. "Of course not. My goal since the minute you saw me and Genn has been to get you back!"

I can't blame her for being mad. I had to know, though. I nod in acceptance and she relaxes.

"I want you and I'll do whatever it takes. Now that this tour is almost over, I can focus on my life again. Can we start over? Can we start us again? Even if it has to be at the beginning?" Her anger is gone and now she just looks vulnerable and defeated. I want to snuggle up to her.

We hear Hannah moving around and making noises so Ali goes into the bedroom and comes back with the cutest little girl I've ever seen. She looks just like Ali and my heart almost breaks. She sits down and Hannah curls up in her arms, too shy to look at me.

"Hannah, this is my friend, Beth. Can you say hi?" she asks. Hannah peeks out from Ali's shoulder and smiles at me. She whispers something in Ali's ear and Ali smiles. "I think she looks like a mermaid," Ali says. Hannah's eyes get really big. "Do you think so, too?" Hannah nods.

"It's nice to meet you, Hannah. You look just like your Aunt Ali." She smiles at me. "Did you have fun at the zoo today?" That piques her interest. Suddenly, we're best friends and she's standing on the couch between me and Ali telling me all about the alligators and giraffes and how the hippos were blowing water at them.

"Hey, hey, Hannah. Let's go see Mom. She's been asking where her little angel is, and I have no idea who she's talking about," Ali says. I smile at Ali's teasing. Hannah squawks and points to herself. Ali teases her some more and then scoops her up and whisks her out the door. She leans back and tells me she'll only be a minute. I nod and she disappears. I'm glad because I need a moment. We got to the heart of the matter in such a short time, and I just need a break. I lean back on the couch and relax.

True to her word, Ali's back within a minute. Now it's just us in the room and I'm tired. I'm tired of worrying and stressing if I'm going to find happiness with Ali. My life is unique. I need somebody who fits me and respects what I do. Ali sits down closer to me this time and reaches out for my hand.

"Your niece is a doll." I'm trying hard not to focus on her running her long fingers over mine, but I'm failing miserably. I close my eyes for a second and recall how incredible those fingers were on my skin and how alive they made me feel. She's only touching my hand, but the rest of my body is stirring.

"I love her to death. She's one of the reasons I can't wait to get home and be done with this tour," she says. I realize Ali will always want to live near her family. I don't blame her one bit. If I had a family as large and supportive as Ali's, I wouldn't want to leave them either. "So what do we do now?"

I stare at her, surprised I can maintain eye contact.

"Let's see where this goes." My voice is quiet. She squeezes my hand and I can't help but smile. "I can visit whenever you want. We're going to make this work, okay?" She brings my hand up to her lips and kisses it gently. She rests her head back on the sofa next to mine. I can tell she's tired.

"Why don't you get some sleep and I'll just see you tonight," I say. She walks me to the door after I assure her I'll be fine getting to my hotel room at three in the afternoon. I feel her so close behind me. If I stop, she'll crash into me. A part of me wants that. I want to feel her body against mine. I turn to face her, not sure how we're supposed to say good-bye.

"Are we allowed to touch?" she asks me, her arms out

for a hug but still close to her sides. I nod and practically sink into her. We move past the point of hugging until we're simply holding one another. She's shaking and I look up at her. She's silently crying. I hold her tighter.

"I'm so sorry. I'm so sorry," she says. I know she's really broken up about this. I softly rub her back and quiet her until she's breathing normally again.

"I know you are. Tomorrow we start fresh, okay?" She nods. I kiss her cheek before I leave the room.

CHAPTER TWENTY-SEVEN

The concert is amazing. I'm backstage again, but this time for the entire show instead of just the encore. Ali is fantastic and I can tell she loves what she does. The crowd is happy to be there, to be a part of her final concert. I'm so thankful that I sucked it up and called her and am sharing this with her. I can't find her family in the crowd, but in all fairness, my attention is on Ali. She's messed up a few times and looks my way every time she does. I know she's playfully blaming me. Brian throws his drumstick at her, berating her lack of concentration. She plays it off by getting the crowd to boo him.

"Thank you so much for sharing this incredible night with me, San Diego. Thanks to my family who is here tonight. They have always helped and supported me. It's been a great tour and I appreciate all of you coming out." She waves and skips offstage right toward me. I know I have that cheesy grin on my face that I get around her. She stops about a foot in front of me, and I can't help but close the gap and give her a quick hug.

"You really are incredible onstage, you know that?" She smiles at me, then grabs a bottled water and drinks half of it right away. I'm glad tonight is her last concert because she's getting hoarse and needs a break. She quickly wipes the sweat off her neck and forehead and then heads back onstage with the band. They play two more songs, getting the crowd back on their feet. I can tell Ali and the band are out there having a good time because this will probably be the last time they're all onstage for a while or even ever again. I was surprised to find that solo artists tour with pick-up musicians quite a bit. I was just starting to like Brian, too. I hope he ends up playing with her in the future. He's good and their camaraderie is entertaining.

Once Ali is offstage, she heads for me again.

"I know you're not ready to meet my family just yet, but would you be willing to have a drink with me down in the lobby of your hotel after I get cleaned up?" She sounds hopeful and happy. I can't turn her down. I nod and she smiles that perfect smile. She tells me she's going to meet with her family for a minute but promises to be in my lobby in an hour.

Ali has arranged for a car to take me back to my hotel, which isn't far from the venue. I have time to get presentable and have a drink to calm my nerves. Now it'll just be the two of us. No Hannah, no Hart family. I'm nervous.

I still look good so I freshen up and head downstairs. I feel somewhat exposed because I'm a single woman in a bar after midnight, ordering a drink. I can't do this alone so I start talking to Em. Anything to get my mind off sitting here alone. She doesn't mind waiting. Love is just on the other side, she points out. That's too close to what I'm feeling so I change the subject because I'm not ready to go there yet.

I feel Ali walk into the bar before I see her. I don't understand how I know she's close before I lay eyes on her. I turn my head and stare right at her. We look at each other for a few seconds before she breaks into a smile.

"Hi. I'm sorry I'm a few minutes late," she says. I shake my head because I didn't even notice. She sits down and our waitress is there ready to take her order. She orders a gin and tonic and a large water. I'm sure she's dehydrated after her performance.

"I'm glad you're here." I don't hide the fact that I'm checking her out. She's still wearing her concert clothes, but her long hair is now pulled away from her face. She has such a beautiful face with her high cheekbones and bedroom eyes. I could stare at her forever. "The concert really was great." She smiles at that.

"As incredible as this tour was, I'm glad it's done." She leans back in her chair and her shoulders slump as she allows herself to relax. "Now I get to go back to my life, but first I need to decompress." I know Ali's going to the spa with her mom and her aunt on Sunday night for a week.

"You deserve it, Ali," I say. She closes her eyes, sighs, and smiles.

"I can't wait. They have the best natural-spring baths and massages, and I refuse to do a thing. I might even have my mother spoon-feed me."

"How was the family tonight?"

"They had a great time. It's always good to wrap up my tour with them. They've been seeing a lot of San Diego. Half of them almost fell asleep during the concert." She's kidding. Nobody could have fallen asleep through that. We talk about the concert and she tells me her favorite things and I tell her what I enjoyed. I skip the part about how I couldn't take my eyes off her or how I was itching to touch her.

"How long are you in town?" she asks. Her smile disappears.

"I'm scheduled to leave Sunday."

"I'd like to spend more time together tomorrow, if you want."

"I wouldn't be here if I didn't want to be. I just don't want to take time away from your family."

"I live with them. They see me all the time." She checks her watch. "I do have to go to a bar tomorrow night. Not to sing or anything, just to hang out. I'd love it if you went with me." She sounds hopeful.

"I'd like that, too."

"It's getting late. Why don't you call me in the morning when you wake up and we'll plan a time." She's probably exhausted and needs rest so I don't protest. She reaches out for me and I go to her. So much for baby steps. I'm okay with that. She kisses my head and releases me. "Do you want me to walk you to your room?" I nod and we walk to the elevators, my hand tucked into hers. I am getting that jittery feeling in the pit of my stomach. I'm afraid I'll be weak when we get to my door and do something foolish like rip off my clothes or, worse, rip off hers.

She's perfectly respectable and gently kisses my cheek before turning and walking back down the hall after dropping me off. She looks back at me once and gives me a quick wave. I'm surprised and somewhat disappointed that she didn't press to stay.

CHAPTER TWENTY-EIGHT

I'm not surprised when I hear tapping on the door. Ali left ten minutes ago, but something makes me think she's back. I want the knock to be Ali. Desperately. Without even looking, I open the door.

"I don't want to leave. I want to stay here with you." A very vulnerable Ali stands in front of me. "You came here for me and I just don't want to go. I'm afraid if I do, you won't be here tomorrow. Can I stay? I'll sleep on the other bed. I just want to be near you."

My heart jumps and threatens to spill out right there between us. I'm wearing pajama shorts and a tank top, toothbrush in my hand, and I couldn't be further from sexy if I tried. I want to throw myself at Ali, but instead I push the door open farther and motion for her to come in.

"I'm so tired," she says, resting her head in her hands. I sit across from her, on my own bed. I want to comfort her, but I'm afraid any more contact will set us spiraling into a bout of passionate sex. I can't handle that right now.

"Why don't you go take a shower? You might feel better after that. You'll probably sleep better," I say. "I can give you something to sleep in."

She's quiet, her head still in her hands, her expression

hidden from me. Finally, she nods and heads straight for the bathroom. I quickly dig through my clothes to find a pair of shorts and a T-shirt. I knock on the door softly and slip inside, putting the clothes on the shelf where she'll find them.

I don't want to look at Ali, but I can't help it. The shower curtain is frosted two-thirds of the way down, but I can see her head and shoulders. She's leaning forward, hands pressed against the wall, the water beating down on her. She looks so alone. I just want to shed my clothes and join her and tell her it's going to be okay. I leave instead because I don't even know if that's true.

When Ali emerges from the bathroom, our eyes meet and I feel the jolt again. She always takes my breath away. Even beaten down and exhausted, she's still as beautiful as the day we met.

"Did that help?" I ask her. I'm leaning up against the headboard, dead center, my laptop on my thighs with a few papers surrounding me. I'm sure Ali thinks it's a fortress, but I really am working. I have an idea for another book and, with Ali this close to me, I'm going to have a hard time sleeping.

"Yes, it did. Thank you for taking care of me," she says. She pulls back the covers of the other bed and slides between the sheets. She rolls on her back and covers her eyes with her forearm. I quietly gather up the stacks of paper and my laptop and put them on the desk. Ali doesn't move. In a way, I'm disappointed. I thought for sure she'd somehow work her way over to me. She hasn't even budged from her spot.

I turn off the lights and try to figure out what's going on. Our initial meeting today was intense, but we both pushed through the uncomfortable and unknown feelings. I try to make out Ali in the dark. I hear her steady, even breathing and know she's asleep. I miss her. I've been miserable without her. I miss talking to her late at night. I miss hearing her seductive voice.

I miss hearing her sultry laugh and the way she whispers my name. Now that she's done with her tour and I'm done writing, we can work on us. My edits won't be too demanding, I hope. I don't mind. I love the characters I've created and miss them like I do real people. It's sad that I still have imaginary friends at age thirty.

❖

Ali's moans jar me awake. I stop and listen, my body on high alert. Did I imagine the noise? A few seconds later, I hear Ali again.

"No…please don't," she says. She's starting to get louder and moving around in the bed more.

"Shh, Ali, it's okay," I say. I want to soothe her but not wake her. Without hesitating, I slip into bed beside her and hold her. She stills and her breathing evens out. I know I should move back into my bed, but I don't want to. I just want to hold Ali for a little bit longer. There's no harm in that. I want to feel her against me and smell her and feel her warmth. God, I missed this. I'm aware of the intensity of my feelings for Ali. One minute I'm wallowing in self-pity and the next I want to fall down at this woman's feet and pledge my eternal devotion. I don't know if this is love or not. It feels more intense. I've never felt this way. I know I should be disappointed in myself, in my lack of conviction, but I'm way past that. I'm an addict when it comes to Ali Hart.

When I open my eyes sometime later, I'm surprised that I'm still in bed with Ali. During the night, Ali rolled onto her back and now I'm tucked into the crook of her arm. My hand is settled under Ali's T-shirt, my fingertips resting on her warm stomach. My leg is nestled between hers, and I can feel the warmth of her core against my thigh. I freeze. How the hell am I going to get out of this? Then I ask myself if I want to get out of this. As I'm trying to answer my own questions, I start rubbing Ali's stomach with my fingers. I stop and rest them flat down against her stomach again.

"I can tell that you're awake," I say. I'm not going to jump and run to my bed. I'm caught, but I don't even care at this point.

"How can you tell?" Ali asks. Her voice is gravelly and sexy.

"Your heart started beating faster and you have goose bumps," I say. We're both silent for a few seconds. "Is this okay?"

"I don't want you to stop. Ever," she says. Her arm tightens against me and I melt into her. We hold each other quietly, both of us aware of the magnitude of this moment. Thousands of unspoken words hang between us, but we're content to communicate via small touches. I resume touching Ali's stomach and catch my breath when I hear her moan softly. She runs her fingers up and down my arm. I feel the pressure of Ali's lips against my forehead as she kisses me softly.

"As much as this pains me, I need to get up and go to the bathroom. I feel like I've been asleep for days," she says. I begrudgingly untangle myself from her long limbs, missing her heat immediately. I sit up and allow her to slip by me, watching her in the dark as she makes her way to the bathroom. Should I head to my own bed? I'm not sure what to do. I end up staying right where I am.

CHAPTER TWENTY-NINE

I should feel relaxed. I'm out in San Diego on a Saturday night at a very nice restaurant with a beautiful woman. We're drinking wine and eating a fantastic dinner, but I'm restless. This electricity between me and Ali is almost unbearable. A static charge is bouncing back and forth between us, and even though we agreed to take things slow, I have this incredible urge to jump her. I want that feeling of losing control again. Of giving it to her and seeing where she takes me. I'm watching her mouth, how wet her lips are as she sips her wine and takes bites of her pasta. I know I'm looking at her hungrily, but at this point, I don't care. I'm on my third glass of wine and I'm feeling pretty good.

"Oh, Beth, what's on your mind?" she says. She busts me. I want to be embarrassed, but I'm not. I smile at her over the rim of my glass. I need to settle down. I don't want to have any doubts when we do finally have sex again. I don't want to regret it. I've already forgiven her, right? So why am I punishing myself by holding out?

"Nothing." I try to sound nonchalant but fail miserably. "So, tell me about the club we're going to tonight. How do you know these people?"

"Well, John gave me my first break, but Mica gave me

the opportunity to sing in a gay and lesbian environment. My songs aren't gay per se, so John didn't have a problem letting me sing. But Mica gave me the stage several nights a week as I was getting started. Whenever I'm this way, I stop by. Plus, she asked me."

I respect Ali and her professional ambition. She also never forgets where she's from. I've met some real snobs in this world who've been blessed with fortune and fame, and Ali's nothing like them. I'm excited to see how Ali handles us out together. We've only been on a few dates.

"Are you ready?" Ali asks. I'm surprised to feel the effects of the wine. I can always tell I've had alcohol because my legs feel funny. Some people get dizzy, my legs feel weak. Ali reaches out to steady me and I giggle. What's wrong with me? I never giggle. She wraps her arm around my waist and escorts me out of the restaurant. She feels so warm and strong, and I can't help but lean into her. We stand outside waiting for a cab, and she kisses me softly and quickly. Oh, how I've missed her lips. Her soft, full red lips.

"I'm sorry. I just couldn't help it. It amazes me how little self-control I have around you." She bends down and kisses me again, barely running her tongue across my lips. This kiss shakes me. Ali is confident tonight.

I sigh and break the kiss. I reach up and gingerly touch her lips, feeling their silkiness under my fingertips. She smiles and pulls back.

"That tickles," she says. I giggle again. I mentally smack my forehead. Em and Shakespeare shake their heads at me. I'm not a seductress tonight. Not by a long shot. Hell, I can barely pronounce the word. I mentally recite it until Ali's looking at me like I've lost my mind. Thank God the taxi pulls up to save me from an embarrassing explanation. We slip inside and we're off. We snuggle in the backseat, and I'm so close to her,

I'm practically on her lap. I shouldn't be so open with her, but then again, she's not fighting me. She holds my hand in hers, running her thumb over the back of it. I love her hands on me. I love the way she speaks to me through touch.

"Before we were together, I had to stop myself from touching you every time you were near me. Do you remember when you fell and Val grabbed you before I could? I still wanted to reach out for you. Isn't that crazy? Every time you were within reach of me, you turned away and went somewhere else. It drove me nuts," she says.

"I had to keep my distance. You frightened me," I say. She seems surprised.

"Really? I mean, I remember you said you had to keep your distance, but I didn't think you were scared of me."

"Just by my feelings for you. They overwhelmed me. I wasn't ready for them or you."

"Are you ready for me now?" she asks.

"I'm here," I say. She kisses me again.

"I couldn't be happier," she says. I could be, if we were back at the hotel room naked. She leans back and smiles sexily at me. I swear sometimes she can really read my mind.

"I have a feeling I'm going to have to fight off a lot of beautiful women tonight," I say. I'm pouting. She laughs. "Okay, let's look at the facts. You're a beautiful, successful singer who makes incredible music and everybody knows you and loves you. I'm going to be jealous all night long."

"This will be our first night together where we can be ourselves. John's place was fun, but there weren't any gay people there. And we weren't together at the girl-to-girl thing down at camp. Tonight will be interesting," she says.

"Well, I think it will be wonderful," I say. "I want to get you somewhere where I can kiss you in front of everybody so there isn't any doubt that we're together," I say. She gives me an odd look and I think maybe I crossed the line. Ali remains silent, and I know I'm going to have to explain myself better. "I'm not sharing you, Ali. I'm not going through what I went through before," I explain, trying to keep the anger out of my voice. "I just want you to be true to me and I'll do the same."

Ali leans forward, inches from my face. "I'd give up everything for you. Being apart from you nearly destroyed me, and there's no way in hell I'm going through that again. I'm not a player and haven't been for a very long time. Now it's just a matter of trust," she says, a mixture of anger and passion in her look. I gulp. Yep, tonight's going to be interesting.

Ali leans back and looks at a text. It's Mica giving us instructions for when we arrive. We pull up to the Koala Bar and make our way to the front of the line. The closer we get to the door, the more I can feel the music thumping in my chest. The bouncer motions us in. I smile at the wolf whistles and ignore the barbs from disgruntled partygoers still lined up outside. Ali pulls me in front of her as we walk through the door. A large woman with short, spiky gray hair approaches us and gives Ali a hug. Ali smiles and winks at me.

"Mica, this is my girlfriend, Bethany. Bethany, this is Mica." She smiles at both of us.

"Nice to meet you, Mica," I say. I'm so happy that Ali called me her girlfriend. Yes, I believe I'm still tipsy.

"She's beautiful, Ali. Does she have an older sister?" Mica asks. She playfully winks at both of us. She shoos us inside and points to the V.I.P. lounge upstairs. We nod and head that way. The music is so loud that talking is no longer an option. When we make it to the V.I.P. room, it is quieter. The heavy, thick, velvet drapes around the room must keep a lot of the noise down. I walk to the windows that face the dance floor and look at all the people dancing. Ali walks over to me and hands me a water. I guess I'm done with alcohol for the night.

I turn back to the crowd. It's warm in here, but I don't know if that's the room temperature or the fact that Ali's right behind me looking over my shoulder at the crowd. I can hear her humming and I close my eyes. I'm so happy right now. I remember the last time we danced. That started us. As if reading my mind, she slides up behind me, intimately, no space between us. Her fingers splay across my stomach. It's an intimate touch and I love it. It's possessive and domineering. Or maybe that's the alcohol and the music and the fact that I'm dying for her to touch me. She starts slowly moving with me, her hips against mine, and I want to beg her to make me come.

"I'm going to find Mica so we can get out of here," she says. She growls in my ear. Before she has a chance to go anywhere, a group of women make their way into the lounge. They start squealing the minute they see Ali, and I know our moment of intimacy is over. She kisses me on my temple and goes over to her mini fan club.

I pout for a second or two, then take the time apart from Ali to collect myself. My body's humming with need. I've never felt this sexual with another person before. Why do I have this incredibly deep connection with Ali? Is it because she's a musician and radiates sex? Is it because I've hit my peak at thirty? I'm definitely more brazen with her. Maybe she knows exactly how to release this side of me, tiny steps at a time so I'm not overwhelmed.

I give Ali and her fans space and walk over to the bar. I'm tempted to ask for a drink, but instead I ask for a Coke. Caffeine and cold. I'd rather have coffee, but I don't think I'm going to get that here. More and more people are entering the V.I.P. lounge.

"Why are you over here?" Ali asks.

"This is your time with your fans," I say. I think it's pretty obvious that I'm giving her space.

"No, we're here spending time together and they just happen to be here." She winks. She pulls me gently into her arms and takes me over to a table where Mica and her partner are sitting. I scoot into the booth, Ali right at my hip, and smile when she puts her arm around me. She quickly introduces me to some of the elephants and they smile at me, but I know they hate me. I want to giggle behind my hand like a little girl, but I refrain. This is a big step for both of us and I should try being mature.

Everybody's talking about Ali's success and I know I should pay attention because this is who she is, but I feel myself slipping away because I don't know these people. Besides, the lure of chatting with Emily right now is too strong. I'm realizing that alcohol really does blur the line between reality and fantasy. It's a lot easier to glide into my imaginary world after three glasses of wine. I'm surprised Em is scolding me for drinking. Apparently I haven't been the model of etiquette tonight, and she's not used to me drinking in excess. Perhaps Shakespeare will be more forgiving. It'll be a good half an hour before I crash into my conservative self again so I might as well enjoy this feeling and share it with somebody who appreciates fine liquor.

"We have one more stop to make, Mica, so we need to get going," Ali says. She grabs my hand and pulls me with her out of the booth. Finally! Ali says good-bye to Mica, Mica's partner, and the elephants, and we walk out into the night. The line to get in is still long and people recognize Ali. While we wait for our cab, Ali poses for photos with some fans. I'm amazed at how gracious and nice she is to complete strangers. I tend to run the other way if somebody yells my name.

"That was quite the night," I say. I snuggle up to her as she gives the driver our hotel address and sigh when she puts her arm around me again. I've missed her so much. We're quiet on the ride back. I'm enjoying the drive and Ali's checking her mail on her phone. I don't blame her, though. She's a very busy person, especially since the tour ended and she's helping Maureen process money and figuring out paychecks and other miscellaneous expenses. When we arrive at the hotel, I slide out and reach for Ali. I want her with me tonight. Tonight we continue celebrating us.

CHAPTER THIRTY

A li takes the key from me because I'm too nervous to find the slot and she has steadier hands.

"Are you sure about this?" She turns me to face her and I nod. I'm so ready to touch her and be touched. She pushes the door open, and as soon as we're through, she pulls me to her and we start kissing. It's sweet, but I want passion. I know she's being gentle with me because this is a big step for us, but at some point, I'm going to have to get bossy. We head over to the bed and she unzips my dress as I kick off my shoes. I slide off her jacket and start unbuttoning her shirt. We fall back onto the bed, and for a second I'm excited because she's on top of me and her weight feels wonderful between my legs. She lifts herself off me and I frown at her absence.

"Where are you going?"

"I want to look at you." She smiles. I suddenly realize every single light is on and she really can see everything. I want to cover up, but I want her to see me, too. I wish we could compromise and leave one light on across the room. She props up on her elbow and slowly traces her finger down my neck. I like that. My neck's extremely sensitive. She traces the strap of my bra, her fingers lightly outlining the lace. My nipples harden and I pray that she gives them attention, too.

She is taking her time and I'm going crazy. She's very serious so I decide a few more minutes won't kill me. She moves closer to me and begins tracing the lace with her tongue. I arch into her but keep my hands to myself. She alternates between fingertips and her tongue. Watching her is very erotic. Her eyes are partially closed as she continues to kiss and touch me. I can see what she's going to do next, and my body tightens in anticipation. I can feel the heat of her mouth through my bra and lean into her when her mouth hovers above my nipple. Finally, finally she pulls down the lace and sucks my nipple into her mouth. Her warm, wet, wonderful mouth. My moan is a half scream, and I don't know if it's because she's finally sucking my nipple or from frustration at her tenderness. She moves back up to kiss me and I melt. Her kiss is still gentle and I know she's holding back.

"Take control," I say. She stops and looks at me, seeming confused. "Take control of me. Make. Me. Yours." I say each word slowly, hoping she'll understand me. She doesn't move for a second or two and I think I've said the wrong thing when she's suddenly between my legs again, her weight pressed into me, her hands pushing mine above my head. "Yes," I say.

That's the last coherent thought I have for a solid minute. My senses are on overload as I taste her, smell her, feel her body touching mine. Her hands are on my wrists, and her upper body weight is pressing down on me. I'm completely helpless, but I've submitted to her already and I'm anxious for her to continue. She leaves me for a moment and I'm devastated. She takes off her clothes. She's so beautiful and I want to reach out and touch her, but I'm pretty sure I'm not supposed to move. Even if I could, I'd need a few seconds for the blood to reach my hands. She stands above me, by the side of the bed, and reaches down to pull off my bra. It's a front clasp and she's not too gentle about it. I bite my lip because she's kind of rough and it's hot. She reaches down and runs her thumb across my lip.

"Save the biting for me, love." Christ. Just her words can almost bring me to orgasm. She runs her fingers over my body, rubbing my breasts with both hands, pinching the nipples just hard enough to make me moan. Her hands move down my stomach until they reach my thong. She puts her hands inside the tiny strip of material on either side of my legs. I'm praying that she rips them off, but she does something completely new, and, for the first time, I'm second-guessing my command. She grabs my hips and flips me over. A move any wrestler would be proud of. Suddenly, I'm on my stomach and I'm not quite sure what's going to happen next because her body isn't on top of mine.

"Do you trust me, Beth?" she asks. I look back at her and we stare at each other for a few moments. She's poised and waiting for my answer. There's so much to that question. I close my eyes. Of course I trust her. I'm trusting her with my body and my heart. Am I ready for this? I open my eyes.

"Yes." That one word means so much. She knows it and nods. I turn back around when we break eye contact. I feel her tongue on the back of my thighs and inhale sharply. I'm so sensitive that I find it hard to catch my breath. She spreads my legs apart as her tongue moves closer and closer to my pussy. The thong is rubbing on my clit and I'm trying very hard not to come. She must realize this because she stops and slides the thong down my legs. She licks my slit and I automatically lift my hips up to give her better access. My face is buried in the pillow to hide my gasps and moans of deep pleasure. She runs her hands over my ass and follows the path with her tongue.

I try not to tense up, but I can't help it. The feeling takes my breath away. I clutch the sheets, pulling them up as her tongue continues to torture me. I can't even form a word.

Her fingers find my wet pussy and slide inside. Now, I'm on my elbows grinding against her hand. She moves up to my shoulder and bites my neck as her fingers thrust in and out of me. I know I'm being loud, but I can't help it. This is exactly what I meant when I told her to control me. I feel her body behind me pushing her hand inside me, and I spread myself even wider. My head is banging against the headboard and I have to hold my arm out in front of me against the wall to steady myself.

"You're mine," she says. "Only mine." Her mouth finds my neck again and starts sucking. Harder this time. I have no idea how she can touch me in so many different places at once, but I hope she never stops. My orgasm is building and I want to be greedy and keep this feeling forever. We have all night so I embrace it and let it crash over me. I'm so engulfed in this moment, I want to cry. I'm shaking, sweating, and overwhelmed by my release. I sink down, my body still riding tiny waves of aftershocks. She curls up behind me, her arm around me possessively. "Did I hurt you?" she asks. I raise myself up on wobbly elbows and turn to face her.

"Are you kidding? That was incredible. I want to do it again." I'm still out of breath. She smiles at me with her sexy, confident smile. I press into her and kiss her hard. She tastes like me and I moan at the familiarity. I'm still weak, so I fall back onto the pillow but bring her down with me. We're still kissing and I move my hand between us. Her boy shorts are crumpled and soaking wet. I just want to dive into her. I yank on her underwear in an effort to get her to take them off, and she moans at the contact. My body is suddenly alert again.

"Take these off," I say. She quickly obliges. I can't wait to touch her. I move my hand back down and slip inside her. I start with two fingers. She moans and bites my lip. She's so wet so I add a third finger, and she breaks our kiss to moan again, loudly. She straddles me to give me full access. She's so tight and I can feel her body gripping my fingers, sucking them in, pushing them out. I wind my other hand into her hair and pull her down to me. She moves her hips against my hand and kisses me, but I want more.

"Come here." I release her hair and pat the bed next to me. She carefully climbs off me. I miss her warmth right away. I seek her pussy out again, this time with my mouth and hands. I need to touch her, taste her, consume her again. I lick her clit, then slam my fingers into her over and over. She starts moving her legs back and forth. That's the signal that she's close to release. I want to stop and build her back up, but I'm so desperate to pleasure her that I don't. I let her come hard, fast, and loud. She surprises me by coming twice. I'm giddy and sleepy. She's quivering beside me, her arm over her face.

"You're wonderful," I say. She uncovers her eyes and looks down at me.

"That was incredible. I've missed you so much." She hugs me with what little energy she has left, squeezing me closer to her. We lie there like that, neither of us speaking, until I hear her breathing even out and know she's asleep.

CHAPTER THIRTY-ONE

My phone rings at two thirty a.m. Immediately, I'm on high alert. I sit up in bed and grab it. It's Ali.

"Ali? Are you okay?" My heart is hammering.

"I'm fine. Sorry I woke you. I was hoping you'd still be awake." Her voice is gravelly and low, and I relax. I don't want to tell her that I've been asleep for about two hours because then she'll want to hang up.

"It's okay. I just went to bed." I'm trying not to sound groggy. I know there's a time difference between Phoenix and Chicago, but I can't do the math right now. She's been at the spa for three days, relaxing and enjoying much-needed pampering.

"I couldn't sleep because I kept thinking about you. Our weekend was perfect," she says. Her voice is low and thick. Has she been drinking? I smile and don't know why. Yes, our weekend was incredible, but I can tell she's somewhat off. Maybe not totally drunk, but definitely tipsy. I wonder if she'll remember this in the morning. I decide to play with her.

"Oh yeah? Tell me what was perfect about it." I can't believe I'm saying this. I don't know where my boldness is coming from.

"The way you taste. Everywhere. Perfect." I can hear

her smile and my stomach flip-flops. God, she's so good with words. "I wish I could wake up and have you here. Then I could wake you up…like I did…remember how I woke you up our first time?" Christ, do I remember. Best sex I ever had.

"Oh, I remember," I say. My voice is getting low, too. I lie back down on the bed now that I know everything's fine and she just misses me. I want to tell her that she consumed me our first night. That she awakened my libido and did things to me I never expected to experience, but I can't tell her yet. I'm far too reserved. I'm not very good at losing my inhibitions and being playful. Our relationship is just too fresh.

"I can't even tell you my favorite part," she says. Her voice is slurred and it makes me smile. "Oh wait! Yes, I can." She's excited now. "When you weren't wearing any panties. That night. Mmm! That was so sexy, Beth. No, wait. When we were on the floor and I was dressed and you weren't and you were on my lap. Mmm. Yeah, that was my favorite."

At this point, my whole body's on fire. I'm completely tense because I can't believe she's talking so openly. She sounds so sexy and I'm transported back to our weekend.

"What did you like? Did I do everything right?" she asks. "I mean, 'cause we can do whatever you want."

I'm not sure if she really wants me to answer or if she's aware she's even asked me questions.

"Really, Beth. Was everything okay?" Okay, so she really does want an answer.

"It was perfect. I couldn't have asked for a better weekend." It's simple and easy and answers a lot of questions.

"What was your favorite part? I want to know so I can do it again and again."

I decide to give her a little bit more. "My favorite part was every time you came up behind me and put your hands on my body, I knew exactly what was going to happen."

She's quiet. "I don't understand." Now she really sounds confused. I blame my crappy two-thirty-in-the-morning explanation. Here goes nothing.

"When your hand was high up on my stomach, I knew it was going to be fast and passionate," I say. "When your hands were on my hips, I knew it was going to be slow. And I loved both ways." I know she's going to want to know which style I like more.

"Really? I do that? Hmmm." I can tell she's thinking back and I don't want her to think back further than me.

"The first time you touched me was pretty incredible."

"You're so soft." She sighs. That's not what I meant by her touching me, but I let it go.

"So are you."

"And you're so wet. How are you so wet?" And we've gone there again. "I mean, I've never been with anybody like you." I'm torn between self-conscious, uncomfortable, proud, and pissed off that she's comparing me to others during our conversation. I have nothing to say to that.

"Ali, why don't you go to sleep? It's getting late and you need to rest." I do my best to divert her attention from my embarrassingly wet pussy because I don't know if that's a good thing or not.

"It's just so incredible." At least I think that's what she says, but it comes out slurred. "We need to have more weekends together. Weeks. Months." She's getting louder.

"We will. When you get done with your spa. Then we can see each other whenever we want."

"I want to see you now," she says. I can't help but smile. Thank God she's a happy drunk.

"It's only for a bit longer. I promise."

"Do you like to be tied up?" That question comes out of

nowhere. At first I'm not certain what she said. But judging from the way my body just exploded with heat, I'm pretty sure I heard correctly. I'm quiet because I'm not sure what to say. I never gave being tied up a single thought until that first night we were together and she forced my arms up above my head. That was hot. I'd definitely consider letting her.

"Um, well, I've never done that before," I say.

"What? Really?"

"No. Never."

"Then we should do it," she says. I hear rustling around.

"What are you doing?" I ask.

"Getting naked," she says, as if it's normal. I'm stiff with a mixture of excitement and fear. Is she getting naked because she's going to sleep that way or because something else is about to happen? She's quiet for a bit and then I hear her moan ever so slightly. I know what she's doing and she sounds so delicious. A part of me thinks I should give her privacy, but she obviously wants me to listen or else she'd get off the phone. I'm not sure how I should do this.

"Do you want to tie me up or do you want me to tie you up?" I ask, trying my best at sounding sexy at 2:43 in the morning.

"Mmm."

I have no idea what to say. "I think maybe you should tie me up because I loved it so much when you held my hands over my head. That was incredibly hot." I can hear little moans and mews from her. She isn't trying to hide the fact that she's touching herself. "I wanted to touch you, but not being allowed to was an even bigger turn-on." I cringe because I don't know if this sounds sexy or not. I don't know if this is what she wants. I guess it's okay because I can hear her breathing deepen. "And when you bit me on the neck. I never knew that could feel so good." I want to tell her that my body was on fire and my nipples were rock hard after the moment she bit me, but I'm nervous that it won't sound sexy.

"I can't wait to see you again. I like it when you take control of me. I like giving myself to you." My voice is shaky at my confession. I know that once it's out there, I can't take it back. She's moaning so loud now, and I can picture her naked in bed, her hair spread on the pillow, her thighs spread out as she plays with her clit.

"Oh, Beth. Yes, yes." She's half-moaning. I'm clutching my phone, straining to hear every sound on the other end.

"You're so close." I don't realize I've said it aloud until she responds.

"Oh, God, I am," she says, moments before coming. I'm in total awe of her. That was sensuous and beautiful and I'm afraid to breathe. Holy shit. I'm grinning and I want to groan, but I stay quiet because I'm still listening to her noises. She's still moaning and I can picture her curled up in a ball, her body quivering with aftershocks.

"Why don't you try to sleep now?"

"Okay. Thanks for staying up with me," she whispers. I can tell she's about ten seconds from sleep.

"Good night, Ali." I smile.

Chapter Thirty-two

I'm a bundle of nerves and I keep staring at the clock. Ali's plane landed an hour ago and she'll be here soon. Any minute the doorbell will ring and it'll be the doorman announcing her arrival. I do a quick walk-through again, ensuring my place is spotless. Fresh flowers are in the living room, and I have sandalwood candles burning in the bedroom. When my intercom buzzes, I actually yelp. Ali will be here in my arms in just a few short minutes.

I open the door to a very happy and smiling Ali.

"Hi, there," I say. She drops her bags and reaches for me. We hug until I come to my senses and pull her inside. "How was your flight?"

"It was pretty quick," she says. She kisses me soundly and I'm in heaven. "It's so good to see you." She kisses me again and I moan and lean into her, loving the fit of her long body against mine. She's so warm and soft, and I'm flooded with delicious memories of just a short week ago.

"It's so good to see you, too. Come on in," I say. I take her hand to lead her down the steps.

"Wow. Look at your view," she says. I have floor-to-ceiling windows that overlook downtown Chicago. The furniture on the lower level is arranged so I can look out at the city. "I love this layout." The only room with four walls and a door is the bathroom. The rest of the condo is open space, including the bedroom. "How do you sleep with all this light?" she asks.

I smile and reach for the remote on the coffee table. I punch in a code and a dark-chocolate screen lowers in front of the bedroom area, providing adequate darkness to sleep. It's fashionable enough and gives me the privacy to entertain guests without them having access to my bed.

"Perfect," she says.

"You're probably tired, aren't you?" I ask.

"No, not really." She shakes her head. "It was a direct flight and not that long."

"Let's sit down and get caught up." I point to the couch. "Tell me more about the spa. Did you have fun with your family?"

"It was incredible. My body's relaxed and recovered. I feel as good as new."

"Well, you look and feel fantastic." I blush at my outburst. Ali smiles at me.

"You're so sweet," she says softly, leaning over to kiss me. "And thank you." We scoot closer to one another on the couch. Ali immediately takes my hand in hers. I smile at the gesture. I miss Ali. I miss the simple things that make me realize we're a great couple.

"I have a few things planned. We can do the normal touristy things like visit museums and the planetarium. I'm going to take you to eat incredible food, and we'll go listen to live music just around the corner. There's a great Irish pub and I can guarantee you'll love it." I know how much Ali loves live music. I'm sure she'll want to jump on stage and join in.

"It all sounds great. I'm pretty easy. Whatever you want to do."

"No, this weekend's about what you want to do. You're my guest," I say.

"There isn't much left of tonight so how about we stay in, maybe order some food, and just relax," Ali says. She lifts her eyebrow suggestively. I blush and laugh. She squeezes my hand again.

"Are you interested in real Chicago-style pizza? I know where we can get a really tasty pie." I cringe at my innuendo. "Pizza pie. That's what they call it here." I blush again. Ali bursts out laughing. "Or I can just make a few small pizzas."

"Why don't I help you and we can just make our own? Do you have groceries?"

I snort and cover it up with a cough. I'm pretty sure I bought everything within a five-mile radius. "I stocked up."

"I really love your place. It's so…contemporary. Not what I expected." Ali stretches her hands and runs her fingers along the smooth black-and-gray granite top of the kitchen island. I want those fingers on me again. I promised myself I wouldn't jump Ali the minute she showed up. A part of me loves the wait, while the needy part wants to tear off Ali's clothes and forget about the world for the next several hours. I decide to be sensible instead.

"I love the kitchen. It's my favorite place to be. I can escape from life and everything and just bake and cook and learn. It also keeps me from going stir-crazy," I say. I'm leaning on the counter trying to look as relaxed as possible while my insides are shaking. Ali is here!

I reach for a bottle of wine and offer Ali a drink. We down a few glasses while we make our pizzas. That settles me down. She updates me on a few things happening back in Massachusetts, and I update her on my edits.

"We should celebrate. I don't think we ever did," she says.

"Celebrate what?" So many things are going on it's hard to keep up.

"Finishing your books! I can't wait to read them," Ali says.

She pulls me closer and kisses my temple. We kiss tenderly, at first. Within seconds, our lips are hard against one another. Ali tugs me toward the bed and I stumble with her, excited she wants this as much as I do. We stop when we hear the timer announce that our pizza's done.

"How hungry are you?" she whispers against my mouth.

"The pizza can be reheated." I prefer sex with her over food any day. Reluctantly, I untangle myself from her embrace and head for the kitchen. I'm back in seconds and slide right back into place. We continue kissing until we hit the bed.

"Can the world see us or should we lower the blinds? I want to be the only one who sees you," Ali asks. She starts unbuttoning my shirt.

I stop for a moment and make myself concentrate. I have a habit of forgetting things around her. I tear myself away from her again and find the remote, hitting the button that will hide us from the rest of the world. I turn back to Ali and gasp. She's already removed her shirt and slacks and stands in front of me wearing a lacy black-and-cream bra with matching panties.

"You take my breath away, Ali," I say. I stop and look at her. Her long, smooth legs, her tight, flat stomach, the rise of her creamy breasts are perfect. Her hair's down, the long waves cascading all around her shoulders and down her back. I'm itching to bury my face and my hands in it. She's so beautiful it almost hurts to look at her. "You look incredible."

Ali grabs my shirt and pulls me close to her. She's kind of rough and I kind of like it. It doesn't take long for me to get out of my clothes and strip Ali completely down. It's all a wonderful blur. I run my fingers down her sides, loving the feel of her curves in my hands. She arches into me.

I can feel her trembling, and even though I'm enjoying kissing her, I want more of her. I need to taste her again. I need to feel her come against my mouth and pull my hair and push my face into her. There's a sense of urgency today, probably because we haven't seen each other in over a week.

I trail kisses down her breasts, down her stomach until I'm nestled between her white thighs. She's so pale and soft and I just want to stay here forever. This is my heaven. I run my tongue up and down her slick heat and capture her clit in my mouth. I'm pressed hard against her. I'm holding her hips down because she's bucking them hard against me, and I don't want either one of us to get hurt. Her hands are pressing me into her and I feel her shake. The harder I hold her, the more she moans. I want to be inside her. I slow down and she growls. It turns into an ecstatic moan as I slide two fingers inside her, as far as I can go. She feels tight and tastes warm and tangy. I want to be like this forever, but it's not fair to her so I release her and she comes hard and loud.

"Wow," she says. I smile and place a tiny kiss on her stomach and rest my head right below her breasts. I smile against her sweaty body, happy that she's here with me. She's tangled in my sheets still making little moaning noises at the aftershocks.

"I'd be content just to stay in your condo the entire week, both of us totally naked and doing this every chance we get," Ali says.

"Definitely. Then you'll just have to come back so we can do all the things on my top-ten list of touristy things in Chicago." I turn my head to look up at her. Her eyes are closed and her lips are slightly parted. I can still feel little vibrations running through her body as the orgasm finally settles. She opens her eyes and stares at me.

"I'll do whatever you want," she says. "If you want to go to the zoo, we can, as long as we're together and can find a private spot so I can steal a kiss or two." I smile up at her. She smiles back.

"Now are you hungry for pizza?" I ask. Ali gives me a quick squeeze.

"You know what? I am. Let's go get some plates and have a picnic in bed." She starts to get up, but I gently push her back down on the pillow.

"No, no, no. You're my guest and I'll take care of you and your needs all week." I wink. She laughs.

"What have I done to deserve you?" she asks. I smile as I slide out of bed. "And put some clothes on. I don't want your neighbors to get a free peek." I roll my eyes and pick up Ali's shirt. It falls to mid-thigh and I do a quick twirl.

"Is this all right?" I ask. I bat my eyelashes at her.

"You look delicious."

I head for the kitchen and return with two small pizzas, two empty wineglasses, and a bottle of wine tucked under my arm. We dive in.

"This is the best meal I've had in months," Ali says.

"Oh, just you wait. This is simple. Tomorrow night I have something incredibly yummy planned."

"Well, this is pretty damn good. I'll probably gain five pounds this week."

"I'm sure whatever weight you gain, we will find a way for you to lose it."

We clean up both pizzas and finish off the bottle of wine. I'm still wearing Ali's shirt, but she's completely naked, the sheet draped carelessly across her waist. I could stay like this forever.

❖

We spend the rest of the weekend in bed getting reacquainted. As much as I want her to deepen it with different words, I'm still having a wonderful time. One day she'll understand what words mean to me, but I can't fault her for being careful.

Monday and Tuesday we hit a few touristy places on my list. The good thing about Chicago is that when two women walk down the street holding hands, the world keeps right on spinning and nobody pays attention. It feels good to be out and open with her. I don't want the week to end. Our second chance is proving to be the best decision for both of us. Ali's completely relaxed and dotes on me, and I can feel trust pushing its way back into my heart. I'm surprised it's happening this soon. I thought for sure it would take a while.

Ali's scheduled to leave Thursday night. She has an interview on a morning talk show Friday. She asks me to join her, but I have to be available to Tom until the first round of edits is done, which should be any day now. Technically, I can handle it from New York, but I need to take a step back from us. I love every minute, perhaps too much. I have no idea where Ali is in this relationship. She obviously cares for me and we have incredible sex, but I don't know if it's more. At times I want to tell Ali I'm falling in love with her, but I'm freaked out at the possible consequences of my confession. Ali always speaks her mind, and the fact that she hasn't said anything really meaningful about us makes me uneasy and hesitant to say anything to her.

When Thursday rolls around, we're both very quiet. I sneak out for donuts and coffee and am surprised to find Ali awake, sitting on the couch, watching the news, and waiting for me.

"Bummer. I was going to surprise you with breakfast in

bed and here you are up and ready to start the day," I say. She smiles at me.

"Not really dressed to start the day. I just needed to get up and stretch for a bit," she says. She's wearing capri sweats and a tank top. Her hair's pulled back, exposing her very kissable neck. I take a few precious seconds to stare at her. She looks so young and refreshed, and I know it'll be heart wrenching to let her go. I place a delicate kiss on her lips on my way to the kitchen. Fresh fruit sounds good and so does yogurt. I bustle around and stop. I'm doing stupid busy work to keep my mind off Ali leaving in a few hours. I did this at the cabin, too. I force myself to stop and march back over to Ali. We eat in silence, Ali occasionally touching my arm or my hair.

"I think I'm going to take a shower, if you're done," I say. She nods at me and I clear the plates and make my way to the bathroom. I test the water, strip off my clothes, and slip into the wet heat. A wave of utter sadness hits me and I brace myself against the tiled wall. Ali will be gone in a few hours and I won't see her again until the end of the month. It hurts. God, does it hurt. A few tears escape even though I'm trying not to cry. I stick my head under the water when I hear Ali enter the stall. I hope the water erases my tears.

"This shower thing seems to be a theme with us," Ali says. I give her a soft smile. She senses my sadness because she turns me and holds me tight. "Don't worry. We won't be apart for long. I really want you to come and see me and my family soon. By the end of the month, okay?" she says.

She kisses me reassuringly. I can feel the slow burn inside me building up as Ali starts stroking me. I'm slow to orgasm but quick to fall apart afterward.

CHAPTER THIRTY-THREE

Tonight, I meet her parents. Her entire family, actually. They're throwing a dinner party for me, and I'm so nervous I'm pacing the hotel room. Ali will be here any minute to collect me and I need her strength right now. I've never spent more time getting ready for anything before. I want to look my best. Ali reassures me that it's casual and they're all very relaxed. Her father is a doctor and her mother is an antiques dealer. I pray I don't say or do anything stupid.

The second I hear Ali's knock, I jump and race for the door.

"You look fantastic, Beth," Ali says. Her eyes roam my body. I'm wearing a taupe-colored dress that rests right below my knee, shows off my curves, but is still modest. I'm worried that I'm overdressed, but Ali's wearing very nice slacks and a blouse with a jacket so I sigh in relief. Ali likes how I look, so that boosts my confidence quite a bit. She pulls me to her in a loose hug. "I don't want to wrinkle you, but I need to feel you."

"I'm so nervous, Ali," I say. She smiles and gently kisses me.

"I promise you'll do fine and they'll love you. Let's go or we'll be late." She kisses my nose and slides her hands down my arms. I shiver. How can she turn me from a pile of nerves to a puddle of mush with a simple touch?

The drive is only about ten minutes. Right now, I'm looking out the window, but I'm not seeing the traffic or the houses or trees. I'm deep in conversation with Emily. I need her to give me strength. She needs to push me back into the dinner conversation if she sees me slipping tonight. Ali's parents will probably think I'm crazy otherwise, and I need to make a great first impression.

"It's okay, Beth. I promise you'll have a great time." I don't realize I'm bouncing my leg until Ali reaches over and gently squeezes it. "My family's great. Avery will treat you like she's known you forever. My mom is the sweetest woman on earth, and my dad is charming. And you already know Hannah." She knows that will melt me a little bit. I manage to smile.

"I just want them to like me." I need reassurance even though she's given me enough. I'm surprised that I'm worried. I haven't been worried in a long time.

"Well, you'll have me and Hannah, your best friends, there." She winks. No doubt about that. Just a few days ago, Ali and Hannah had Skyped with me. It was precious. Hannah didn't want to stop talking to me, and Ali tried several times to get the phone away from her. Ali's so good with her, and it's obvious that Hannah adores her. I don't think Hannah knows that her aunt is a famous singer. Of course, your world at four is pretty small, and you worry more about juice, cartoons, and naps than you do about what people do for a living.

"This is true," I say. I try to drum up some confidence.

"Here we are," Ali says. We pull into a very long, curved driveway that is already full of cars. I turn and stare at her openmouthed.

"Are you kidding me? How many people are here?" My voice is getting louder, but I'm on the verge of freaking out.

"Relax. Okay, hang on a minute, let me count." She points at all the cars, counting people in her head, and I stare at her hoping for a low number but knowing it's double digits for sure. "Twenty or so." Her voice drops off as she adds the or so part. I roll my eyes and reach for the passenger-side mirror. My cheeks are starting to turn red. Crap. In about thirty seconds I'll become blotchy. I sigh. Ali reaches down and raises my hand to her lips. "I'll be beside you the entire time, I promise."

I relax a little, but I'm still nervous. She helps me out of the car and I straighten my dress. When I look back up at her, she kisses me softly at first, then with a little more force. For a few seconds I forget where I am. She slows down and breaks away from me. "Ready?" I smile and nod. With just a kiss, she's reminded me why I'm here. A very passionate one, but just a kiss.

"Aunt Ali!" I hear a child squeal. We finally see Hannah worm her way through the parked cars. She crashes into Ali's long legs, wrapping her arms around her thighs. I stand there smiling, watching them. Hannah looks up at me and squeals, "Beth!" and I'm immediately grabbed in the same fashion. I lean down and squeeze her tiny, thin shoulders. She looks up at me with big, brown eyes and I'm under her spell. "You're here! You're here!"

"Hannah, let Ali and Bethany get inside." I look up and see a woman standing in the doorway. She's about my age and looks like Ali, but her hair is shorter and she isn't as tall. Beautiful, but Ali still has her beat. I know she's Ali's sister and Hannah's mom, Jennifer. She smiles and reaches out to hug me.

"It's so good to finally meet you," she says. She sounds so genuine. I smile back at her and thank her for the warm welcome. She grabs my arm and whisks me away from Ali. "Ali and Bethany are here!" Jennifer says. Within a matter of moments, I'm being grabbed and hugged and twirled from family member to family member. This isn't at all what I expected. It's better. When I finally reach her parents, Lucy and Bill, I'm genuinely smiling and not nearly as nervous.

"Bethany, Ali has told us so much about you." Lucy takes my hand and stares at me, squeezing my fingers.

"Yes, she won't shut up," I hear from behind Lucy. Another tall Hart woman appears, putting her arm around Lucy's shoulders. She's obviously Ali's youngest sister, Avery. Adorable, energetic, and still innocent-looking. I understand why Ali's so protective of her. "I'm Avery. It's nice to finally meet you."

Avery looks the most like Ali. She has the same long, wavy hair, but her eyes are more solid brown and she has dimples, the only sibling who does. I can tell right away she's the devilish one in the family. She has a twinkle in her eye, and I can't help but automatically smile at her.

"You're absolutely gorgeous," she says. "Ali wasn't kidding when she said you were beautiful." I'm completely embarrassed so my smile falters. I hate compliments. I thank her and try to move the conversation onto something else. It seems as if suddenly everybody's around me and I'm starting to get a little claustrophobic.

"Give her some room, guys." Ali rescues me. "There's plenty of time to get to know Bethany. We'll be here for a few hours." She hands me a glass of wine and I'm so thankful for something to hold on to, since I doubt Ali will be available the entire time. Half the family scatters, but I can still feel their eyes on me from across the room. "Well, that was the worst of it," she whispers before placing a tiny kiss on my ear. I have to refrain from shivering. She amazes me.

"Come sit down, Bethany." Avery plunks herself on a couch, leaving me plenty of space to sit down. "Let's talk until dinner's ready." I give Ali a small shrug and head that way. As soon as I sit down, Hannah bounces over and lands half on my lap and half on the couch. She's vibrating with energy. "Hey, Hannah Banana. Give Bethany some space," Avery says. I tell her I don't mind, but Hannah scoots over until our legs are still touching, but she's no longer technically on my lap. "So how long are you in town for?" she asks.

"I'll head back on Wednesday. I have a meeting Thursday that I can't miss, or else I'd stay through next weekend," I say. Today's Friday. That gives me five days to get to know Ali's family. So far, so good.

"I started reading one of your books." Avery seems very excited and I can't help but feel her excitement, too. It's always nice to hear that somebody's reading your work. "As a matter of fact, I'm pretty sure a few of us are," she says. She waves her hand around the room. Emily pops up to gloat with me, and we mentally high-five when Avery tells me it's hard to put my book down because it's mysterious and exciting.

Ali's only brother, Mark, takes that moment to come over and introduce himself. I know he graduated college a few years ago and is an engineer at a firm in downtown Boston. He's shy around me but completely comfortable around his sisters. He, too, has wavy brown hair and brown eyes. They're a beautiful family and I'm happy that I finally agreed to meet them.

Bill announces that dinner's ready and Ali escorts me to the table. There are actually two long tables, and Ali takes the chair to Bill's right. She's across from her mother and I'm across from Hannah. This could be trouble. I'll have to refrain from making funny faces at her because I don't think Jennifer would be pleased. I'm still under the first-impression rule where I have to behave. There's a playful fight over who gets to sit next to me, but Avery wins out.

"Trust me, you don't want to sit next to anybody else,"

she says. "They'll either bore you or ask you a ton of questions you don't want to answer."

"But you aren't going to ask me a ton of questions I don't want to answer, right?"

She laughs. "You got me there. I promise to go easy on you." I don't think I believe her. As lively and spirited as she is, I'm sure she's just as protective of Ali as Ali is of her. Her questions don't disappoint me. Unnerve me, yes, but don't disappoint. "So, I know the story of how you and Ali met. Tell me how you, successful writer, beautiful woman, are single?"

And there's the punch to the gut.

"Avery!" Ali hisses over me at her. She looks guilty but shrugs. "You don't need to worry about that." Ali looks angry and I know she's protecting me, but I guess she has a right to know. I place my hand on Ali's arm.

"It's okay," I say. I turn my attention back to Avery. "I was in a long relationship, but it didn't work out. So I went into hiding, licked my wounds, engrossed myself in my writing, and, when I came up for air, Ali was waiting." I'm sure my explanation is acceptable because Avery smiles at me and I can feel Ali relax. Maybe one day Avery will know the full story.

"Aunt Beth! Are you going to the fall festival?" Hannah asks. I'm not sure when I changed from Beth to Aunt Beth, but I'm pretty sure I'll move mountains for this tiny bundle of energy. She's talking to me like I've been around since her birth.

"Can I come, too?" Ali asks. Hannah giggles.

"Of course," she says, matter-of-factly.

The rest of the night goes smoothly. When Ali isn't protecting me from Avery's inquisition, she's deep in conversation with her father. Ali's mother draws me into a conversation about my jewelry. She's been admiring it all night. I explain that my grandmother gave it to me, and I compliment her on her good eye. Most people have no idea that what I'm wearing could probably buy a house. It's very simple, but it's from the 1800s and has been in our family since then. Ali wears her great-grandmother's wedding ring on her ring finger, and it's from the same era. It's nice to know we both like the same kind of jewelry. Lucy invites me to stop by her store, and I find that I really want to.

"Do you know that you're the only woman, besides Gennifer, that Ali has introduced to the family?" Avery asks me, her voice low. I look at her with surprise.

"Wow. No, I didn't." I'm not quite sure what to say to that or how to act. Avery's definitely looking for a reaction, and I'm trying not to smile too broadly. The news really does surprise me. I'll have to ask Ali about that later.

"Yeah, that's why there's such a turnout tonight. I mean, we wanted to meet you because we know this doesn't happen often and Ali is definitely happy." She stumbles over the word happy and I wonder why.

"That's nice," I say. I can see she's somewhat disappointed. I think she wants more of a confession or declaration on my part.

We eventually move back to the living room as some of the family shuffles around to leave. Both Ali and I thank everybody, and I'm kissed and hugged again and again. I'm eating it up. I'm not used to a lot of attention, and who knew I'd like it so much? Hannah has the hardest time saying good-bye. Her little face is red from crying, and Ali promises we'll see her tomorrow at the festival. That perks her up, and she hugs us both good-bye before she sleepily heads to the car. I selfishly want her. She's adorable, potty-trained, and can talk. All the hard stuff is done until the teenage years. Then, I'll gladly give her back until college.

At ten thirty Ali points to the clock. I can't believe we've been here so long. I'm nestled into Ali's side. We're sharing the couch with Avery, who's draped her legs across us. She's as comfortable with us as Hannah is. I'm already in love with Ali's family. I can't believe I didn't want to meet them at her concert. In all fairness, I like this setting better. Ali untangles us and we stand to leave. Lucy grabs me and hugs tight.

"Thank you," she says. I nod. I think she's thanking me for being with Ali, but she could just be thanking me for having dinner. My romantic side says it's the first explanation. It takes us another fifteen minutes before we're in the car. We drive off, and I have a colossal grin on my face.

"Thank you, Ali, that was really nice. You're right. Your family's amazing." I'm completely relaxed. She strokes my cheek. "Please don't kill us." She laughs and looks back at the road. We're back at the hotel in no time. I know I'll be asleep as soon as my head hits the pillow. Ali holds my elbow while I slip off my shoes in the elevator. I want to start stripping as we're walking down the long hallway to my room, but I refrain. I'm leaning on Ali, my head on her shoulder because I'm exhausted. She holds me close and I can hear her hum.

Chapter Thirty-four

Well, we're going to look at houses now," Ali tells Lucy and Avery, who are finishing up the breakfast dishes. This is my second time visiting Ali since her tour ended. I arrived last night and we spent most of the evening touching, kissing, and getting caught up on some much-needed personal time. We reach for our jackets, and I'm startled when Avery shrieks with excitement.

"Oh, my God! You guys are finally moving in together," she says. She starts squealing and jumping up and down. I completely freeze. I don't dare look at Ali. I know we both have the deer-in-headlights look. The elephant in the room keeps getting bigger as the silence grows among all of us.

"No, dork. Bethany's going to help me find a place so I don't have to look at your face every day for the next three months," Ali says. I detect a slight hitch in her voice that does pique my curiosity. Ali's mom shoots me an apologetic look and continues drying the dishes as if the past ten seconds didn't just blow up a grenade of questions that everybody wants answers to.

"We'll see you later this afternoon." Ali steers me out of the door, squeezing my waist slightly as we walk to the car. "Sorry about that. My sister loves you already." Well, at least one Hart does. Ali sends me a heart-stopping smile and, once again, I'm under her spell.

"It's all right. She's adorable and I like her, too." I ignore Ali's exaggerated eye roll. "It's nice to have somebody who's like a little sister to me. Plus, she likes to jog with me while you sleep in." By the end of my last visit, Avery had begged me to run with her after hearing that I jog almost daily in Chicago. I enjoy spending time with her and the rest of Ali's family. I feel like I'm already a part of them.

"Well, if you wouldn't exhaust me every night, then I could get up early and jog with you, too," Ali says. Her joke causes me to blush. She steps in front of me to stop me quickly. She doesn't say anything for a few seconds. She twirls a piece of my hair, lost in some thought she doesn't share.

"I'm just teasing. I wouldn't have it any other way." She gives me a quick hug. "Let's get in the car and warm up." She opens the door for me and I duck inside. I'm shivering because I'm no longer wrapped in Ali's warmth.

"Isn't Chicago pretty cold in the winters, too?" She notices I'm shaking when she slips into the car.

"Yes, but I never have to leave my place. As a writer I can stay inside and be warm for four months if I want."

"But you miss out on the snow and the snow angels and sledding and hot chocolate after playing outside," she says.

"You've been to my place. I'm in the middle of a bunch of skyscrapers. The minute the snow falls, they scoop it up and take it away. I'm sure they'd scoop me up and take me away if I was on the sidewalk making snow angels."

"That's why I want to live around here. Hannah's still young and she loves stuff like sledding. That's the charm of small-town life. I think I'd miss it if I had to live in a big city," Ali says.

Well, at least now I definitely know where Ali stands.

She'd never want to live in Chicago. I completely understand. If I had a large, tight family, I wouldn't want to leave them either. And it's not like we've discussed moving in together or anything.

"Sounds like you like that kind of stuff, too." This is supposed to be a happy time for us since we're together, but I'm not feeling very jovial. Something about this makes me sad. Forcing a smile, I turn to Ali. "Where's the first house?"

We drive about a mile away to a beautiful Victorian. We're early to the appointment so we wait in the car.

"It's lovely, Ali." The house sits on an acre of beautifully manicured land, and I can't help but smile. "It is kind of big, though, don't you think? Or not. I guess I'm just used to my condo." I backtrack, hoping I haven't offended her.

"It is rather grand, isn't it?"

A car pulls up behind us, and Ali waves to a fifty-something woman who looks more like a teacher than a real-estate agent. "Let's see how bad it really is." She winks at me. Introductions are made and we follow Rose up the walkway to enter the foyer.

"Ohhh!" I say. The older architecture completely fascinates me.

"Yes, it's quite charming," Rose says. "It's listed at a reasonable price, but in today's market, if you like it, I'm sure you can make an offer much lower. Shall we look around?"

Ali grabs my hand and we visit each room, commenting on the pluses and minuses. I love the ornate woodwork and touch all the banisters, knobs, and rails. The house is charming, but as we investigate further, we decide the rooms are too small and to tear down the walls to modernize it would take away from its historical appearance.

Ali decides to keep looking and we follow Rose to the next house. It's newer but doesn't sit on a large enough plot of land, and Ali doesn't like how close the neighbors are. When she pulls up to the third house, we look at each other with delight. It's a stunning house, nestled back against beautiful trees on one and a half acres. I fall in love with it instantly.

"Oh, Ali. This is fantastic." I'm enthralled.

She smiles. "It's pretty incredible, huh?"

"It certainly has everything you want and then some. It's not as close to town as the other two, but it's only a few miles away," Rose says.

"It's far enough away to keep my family from just stopping by, but close enough for them to come and see me when they want," Ali says.

"I'm so lost. How far away from your parents' house is this?" I'm completely turned around in this town.

"It's only about a ten-minute drive. That's not bad at all," Ali says. She frowns as she contemplates all the factors. I smile at her face, crinkled in concentration.

"Rose, we'd like to walk around for a bit longer," I tell her. "Do you mind?"

"Oh, no, sweetie. You go right ahead. I'm just going to check in with the office," she says, waving her phone at us. I grab Ali's hand and we review the layout.

"The master bedroom is incredible. It's the size of my condo! You could have your own studio downstairs. It should be easy to soundproof," I say. "I love that it's modern, but the outside has part of the Northeastern charm. What do you think?" I ask her, unable to contain my excitement.

"I think it's great. I'll have to get a report of utilities and taxes and talk it over with my parents. See what they think. Plus, when I'm touring, someone from my family can check in from time to time to make sure I don't have any problems."

"It comes with an alarm system. If you get this house, there really isn't anything for you to do except maybe paint.

Even the garage is move-in ready with shelves and all that dyke stuff."

"Bethany! I can't believe you said that!" Ali laughs. "I barely know a hammer from a screwdriver."

"I'm sure your dad or your brother can help you load the pegboard and get everything you need. And you'll have a three-car garage." I'm excited for her.

"Well, I might have to break down and buy a boat. It can go in the larger bay down at the end. I'm sure the builder designed it with that in mind," she says. "We really aren't that far from the ocean."

"Oh, I love the ocean! Can we go?" It's been a while since I've seen the Atlantic.

"Definitely! I'm sorry I didn't think of that first. Come on. Let's get out of here. I'll tell Rose that I need to do some thinking." Ali grabs my hand. We leave Rose and get back in the car.

"Is it weird that I want to see the house you shared with Gennifer?" I ask.

Ali turns to look at me. "No, not at all. We can swing by if you want."

"Is it close to this house?"

Ali laughs. "No, it's on the opposite side of town. Probably twenty minutes or so from here." Ali drives past her parents' house and jumps on the highway, taking the third exit. After weaving through a quaint, older neighborhood, she slows down in front of a pleasant brick, two-story, bungalow-style house with a wrap-around porch. I'm surprised it's not bigger or newer.

"It's from the turn of the century. The porch was always my favorite thing," she says.

"I think it's cute. You picked out a nice one." I'm not really sure what to say right now.

"It's not as elaborate as the ones we saw today, but I was happy to own something."

"I feel the same about my condo."

"Is it hard to buy and sell condos in Chicago?"

"I don't think so. Tom's son, Brad, rents out my loft in the summers when I'm at camp, and he's been after me to sell it. They can afford it. Even in this economy, I could probably sell it for more than I paid."

"Your condo's very cool. It's funny. The house I'm looking at seems more like you, and your condo seems more like me," she says. "Come on. Let's get back to the house for lunch."

❖

"How was it?" Lucy asks. We shrug off our coats and sit down at the table.

"How was what?" Bill asks.

"They looked at houses today," Lucy says.

"You girls are moving in together? That's great," he says. Again, that same damn question. I can't find Em or Robert anywhere to get me out of here. I simply freeze.

"No, honey. Bethany's just helping Ali find something around here," Lucy says. "And? Did you find anything?" she asks us.

"Well, there is a house about ten minutes from here. It's on an acre and a half and it's move-in ready. Hey, Dad! Three-car garage so I'm thinking it's time for that boat," Ali says. They high-five and he grins the same grin. "Dad and I used to fish on the weekends. It was our special time. Besides, I was the only kid who liked to be outside, get dirty, and hook my own worm. Even Mark couldn't do it," she says.

"Ali, be nice," Lucy says. Ali rolls her eyes and winks at her mom. Apparently, their teasing is normal behavior, but

I'm just not used to it yet. An only child has nobody to tease. "What do you think of the house, Beth?"

"Oh, it's beautiful. It's spacious and warm, and the landscape is perfect. I like that it sits far back from the road and the backyard is private. The deck is fantastic and the kitchen is incredible," I say. I tone it down a bit after I see the look on their faces. Perhaps I'm too excited. "I think Ali will be happy with it."

"You'll have to check it out for me," Ali tells her dad. "Make sure I'm doing the right thing. Plus, according to Beth, you get to help me pick out tools." I reach over and pinch her playfully. "Okay, Bethany wants to go to the beach. We'll probably be gone overnight so don't hold dinner for us."

I look at Ali in surprise. It's already two, and even though the beach is only an hour away, we still need to hit the hotel and pack a quick overnight bag. It gets dark by five thirty so we won't get to see much tonight, but we will first thing in the morning. I'm excited.

"Let's go, love," Ali says. That word causes a jolt to run through my body again. God, I love that feeling. I say good-bye to her family while Ali grabs a bag of clothes. When we get back to my hotel, she makes a few calls while I run up to my room to grab my own stuff. I'm back at the car in a flash.

"We're all set for the night," Ali says. "We are staying at the Seascape Hotel. You'll like it, I think," she says. I wonder how many other women she's brought up here. I force my jealous self to settle down.

"I'm sure it'll be nice. As long as we're together, that's all I care about," I say. Being with Ali's family is great, but I just want to touch her again. I miss her warmth. I want to strum her body to life and listen to her cry out with passion. Ali fell asleep early last night so I didn't get as much time with her as I wanted, and I'm very needy right now. I don't need as much sleep as she does, so I wrote and watched her rest. She's so peaceful in her sleep. She looks innocent and perfect.

❖

The hotel is luxurious and located right on the ocean. We quickly check in and I drag Ali out to walk the beach before sunset. It's a cool fall afternoon, and I can't think of a better place to be with Ali. No one else is on the beach. I reach down and touch the water.

"It's so cold," I say.

"Well, it's mid-November and you're on the East Coast."

"Yeah, but wow. I guess I didn't expect the water temperature to drop so drastically. The weather hasn't been that cold, has it?" I ask. Ali grabs my hands and brings them to her lips. It warms me but gives me the shivers as well. I adore her mouth and the things it does to my body.

"I love that I can read your mind. I know exactly what you're thinking." She narrows her eyes at me.

"Oh, you think so, huh?" I'm challenging her.

"You're thinking that you can't wait to get back to the room so you can have your way with me, right?" Apparently, I'm very obvious. She laughs.

"It's not fair that you can read me like that. I can only tell by your eyes. Sometimes you give me a look that shakes me to my core."

"You have no idea what I'd do for you," she says. I don't know how to process that so I'm quiet. We walk back to the hotel, my head resting on her shoulder, both of us enjoying the simplicity of the moment. I could definitely get used to this. I want to get used to this. Eventually, we'll have to talk about this long-distance romance we're having. At some point, the long weekends will slow down as life catches up with us.

Ali's going on tour in Europe in February. We will have seven weeks apart. Neither of us has mentioned love or a deeper commitment. I've come close to blurting out my feelings, but I figure it'll scare her off. Ultimately, I just want to be with her. I don't care if we never discuss our feelings. I just need her. I need us. That part is scary enough.

We make it up to the room and I realize that Ali has booked the Honeymoon Suite. It's a fantastic room and I take a moment to appreciate it. The view of the ocean is breathtaking. The claw-foot bathtub is big enough for both of us, and Ali suggests a bath. I can't get my clothes off fast enough.

"You know we'll have to order room service because now that you're naked, you won't be wearing clothes again until tomorrow," Ali says.

"I'm still wearing my bra and panties." It's as though I'm wearing nothing. My lacy bra leaves nothing to the imagination, and my thong panties are almost nonexistent.

Ali growls before capturing my mouth in a kiss that leaves us both breathless. I push up Ali's sweater and she pulls it up over her head. I grab Ali's pants and stare into her eyes as I slowly unbutton them and slide them down her long, sexy legs.

"You really are beautiful," I say. I run my tongue along her collarbone and down to the tops of her breasts. I unclasp her bra with one hand and give myself a mental high five for being so smooth. I run my hands over the softness of her breasts, marveling at her perfect body. I shiver at Ali's moans of encouragement and continue running my hands all over her body.

"We need to pick this up after our bubble bath, before the water gets cold," Ali says. She moves out of my grasp. She kisses away my frown and gingerly steps into the steaming tub of bubbles. She reaches out and I quickly join her. After adjusting myself to fit in the curve of her long body, I lean my head back against her chest.

"This is really nice. We fit well together," Ali says. She dabs my hand with bubbles.

"You should get a tub like this for your new house. Or wait. Isn't the Jacuzzi tub in the master suite about this size?" I ask.

"I think so. I hope my dad approves the house."

"Please don't bring up your dad while we're in the bathtub."

She laughs. "You know, my whole family loves you so much. Everybody's happy that I'm happy again. It's been a long time, you know."

"But you and Gennifer only broke up, what, six months ago?"

"True, but we weren't a couple for about six months prior to the official breakup. My family never liked her. They thought she was stuck up and just not nice."

"I can't believe that. I can't believe you'd be with somebody like that," I say. She shrugs.

"I've done a lot of growing up in the last few years. I'm sure that had a lot to do with my decision to end things with her. When we first got together, we were happy and carefree. Looking back, I think we were just young and obnoxious. And rude to my family. People change though. Plus, everybody puts their best foot forward when they first start dating."

"Well, I think we've been pretty honest with each other, right? At least since our talk. But even before that." She kisses my head in agreement. We're quiet for only a moment. I'm relaxing, but I'm pretty sure Ali has something else in mind.

She slides her hands down my body, rubbing gently in all the right spots. I moan as she palms my soapy breasts, then rubs a washcloth across my nipples, the friction driving me crazy. Jolts of pleasure, almost pain, surge through me. I run my hands up and down Ali's leg, squeezing her knees with every jolt. When her fingers find the junction of my thighs, I spread my legs and push my knees against the sides of the bathtub, allowing her full access.

"You're the most passionate person I've ever known." Her raspy voice is low in my ear. Her fingers slowly rub my pussy, spreading me apart. "I love how you feel in my arms and how much you trust me," she says.

I respond by leaning back and kissing her. Our tongues touch and our passion intensifies.

"God, Ali." I moan. I lift my hips up, giving her better access.

"We're getting water all over the floor. Let's go to the bed," she says.

"No, no, no. We're fine. Please." I don't even care that I'm begging at this point.

She continues rubbing me, this time finding my clit in the steamy water.

"Yes…yes…see?" I try to reason with her. I don't want her to stop. I raise my hips up and down, tensing up as she applies more and more pressure. I don't care that my movements are creating tiny waves that splash over the sides. I just need to come. I almost laugh at how selfish I am. I could hold off a few minutes longer and enjoy Ali's hands on me and feel her mouth kissing and biting my neck, but I know we have all night and one selfish orgasm isn't going to ruin it. I push my knees against the side of the tub and come hard. I want to laugh and cry and scream, but I sink back into Ali instead.

"You're incredible," Ali says. I can only breathe deeply and try to calm myself. For a fast orgasm, that was amazing.

God, I could get used to this. This intimacy with Ali is new and exciting, and I want more and more every time we're together. It's getting harder to say good-bye after weekends like this.

Ali coaxes me up and grabs towels for us. We giggle at the amount of water that's outside of the tub, pooling in front of it.

"Let's order room service and continue this over there," Ali says. She points to the king-sized bed. "I believe you owe me several more of those orgasms."

"I believe it's my turn to do delicious things to your body." I grin wickedly at her. I like that I'm getting bold. I figure I might as well have fun with her. We slip on hotel robes and make our way to the bed. Ali uncorks the complimentary champagne and I look at the menu.

"There isn't a whole lot of vegetarian-friendly food on the menu."

"I'm sure they'll make us whatever we want," she says. "Let's find out." She calls room service and orders fettuccine Alfredo and garlic bread. She also asks for chocolate ice cream for dessert because she knows it's my favorite.

"How long did they say?" I ask.

"About twenty minutes." She slides her full length against me on the bed. "What would you like to do until then?"

"I have an idea." I find the knot on her robe and loosen it, exposing her warm body.

"Mmm, I like your ideas."

I kiss her again and she leans up to straddle me. I run my hands down to her hips and pull her up on her knees. Ali smiles against my lips, but then I hear her moan when I find her wet pussy.

"Oh, yeah, I like your ideas a lot," she says.

As soon as I slip my fingers inside, she starts rocking her hips against my hand. I'm in awe of her passion. She knows her body so well and how to move it and get the most out of every thrust and touch. She doesn't hold anything back.

"I love how wet you are right now," I say. She opens her eyes and looks into mine. That look makes me gasp. It's raw and hungry. My confidence grows. "I love how your body molds perfectly to mine, in every way."

Ali crushes her mouth to mine. We don't speak again until she comes. She slows her hips as the waves of passion subside. I gently remove my hand and smile as she collapses on me.

"Well, now I understand why you didn't want to stop in the bathtub," she says. I hold her for all of about thirty seconds until we both jump up at somebody knocking on the door.

Somebody says, "Room service," and we scramble around searching for our robes, trying to cover up.

"This room smells like sex," I whisper. Ali laughs.

"That's what people do in this room!" she says.

She opens the door and allows the server to enter. I look at Ali and smile. She has the I-just-had-sex look. Her hair is tousled, her body still flush with passion. The server smiles at both of us. I can't get him out of the room fast enough.

"He totally knew what we were doing." Ali laughs. I'm embarrassed at having been caught. The openness of our relationship is still very new to me. I've been very private sexually. Because Crystal was in the closet, we were always on our best behavior and never engaged in public displays of affection. At the time, I didn't care, but now I can't imagine not being able to touch Ali or hold her hand whenever I want. It's amazing to me how different Crystal and Ali are. Ali doesn't care if people approve or disapprove of her. She commands attention everywhere she goes and does what she wants, when she wants. I've never advertised my sexuality, but I don't hide it either.

Ali sets up a delicious picnic on the bed and I go over

to her. I have to remind myself to play it cool. She seems so happy with how our relationship is going, and I don't want to tip the scales. Balance is nice. Balance is safe. Balance is boring. I join Ali on the bed, and we rest against the padded headboard and eat.

"Don't forget we have ice cream," I remind her after she clears her plate.

"Somebody made me hungry," she says. She leans down and kisses me. It starts off playfully enough, but soon enough we're pushing our plates out of the way and tearing off our robes.

❖

The next morning comes too soon. I wake up to Ali playing with my hair.

"Hi." My voice cracks and is not sexy like hers.

"Hey there. Good morning," Ali says. She kisses me softly. "I'm surprised to see you still in bed. I never get a chance to see you sleep."

I smile shyly.

"I guess you wore me out last night. What time is it?" I look at the clock. It's just after eight. "Good. We still have most of the day."

"We can either get up and spend the day in town, or…" Ali's voice is lilting and suggestive. I watch her draw patterns on my stomach and trace imaginary circles around my breasts. I love being naked with her.

"Hmm. Our options are limitless." I relax and enjoy her touch.

"But our time isn't," she says.

"Look, Debbie Downer, I don't leave until five. That gives

us nine hours to do anything and everything we want. And I'll see you again in a few weeks."

I notice a faraway look in her eyes. "Hey. Where are you?" I ask.

"Sorry. I was just thinking of things."

"What kind of things?"

"What all I need to do here in the next few weeks. I have the tour coming up. I need to figure out what has to be done," she says. And here I thought she was thinking about me.

"When was the last time you were in Europe?"

"It's been about two years. I think I have more fans overseas than I do here. It should be interesting," she says. "You should come with me."

I try not to jump up and squeal like a little girl.

"I could probably get away for a little bit," I say. I keep my voice calm.

"I'll show you the time of your life," she promises between soft kisses that increase in strength until talking is no longer an option.

CHAPTER THIRTY-FIVE

H ere we are again," Ali says. It's more of a grumble as we walk through the automatic doors at Logan International. "You know how much I hate this." I don't say anything. I squeeze her hand instead.

"I'll be back in a week." I'm trying to be reassuring. I leave her for a moment to check in and dump my luggage. She reaches for my hand the second I return. I love that. "Come on, let me buy you lunch. The flight is delayed thirty minutes. More time together." I'm trying to lighten the heavy mood. I find a small bar and we sit down.

"This is the part I hate. This is when I get to pout and plead for you not to go," Ali says. I can tell she means it.

"I need to meet with Tom and a few of the other editors about the book tomorrow. We're getting close to finalizing everything and then I'm free. Or else I'd stay here." I really mean it. I'd much rather be here. It's getting harder to say good-bye and that surprises me. I've always thought relationships fizzled out after a few months, but we're much stronger now than we ever have been.

I try to keep Ali's mind off the fact that I'm leaving by talking about things that happened over the week. I bring up Avery and how she accidentally slipped into the lake and how

Lucy's dog made us laugh by running figure eights in the backyard. Ali smiles at that. Something about a dog running a continuous path is a riot. I reach out and hold Ali's hand. We fit so well together. I look around the bar. People are looking at us, not because we're holding hands, but because Ali is very popular in the Northeast and people recognize her. This isn't the first time it's happened, but it bothers me more today because Ali's so visibly upset. I hear my flight boarding and tug on her hand.

"Walk me to the gate?" I ask.

"Of course." We walk quietly and slowly to the security checkpoint.

"I always have such a great time with you," I say. She pulls me close and holds me tight. "And I'll see you soon and we can go shopping for your family and you can show me how wonderful the holidays are in a small Northeastern town." I'm trying everything to make her smile. She kisses me softly.

"I love you, Beth," Ali says. It's a whisper, and I'm not one hundred percent sure that's what she just said. She looks sad, but hopeful, and kisses my cheek. I can't move. I take tiny, short breaths. The sounds around me are loud and roaring, and I feel like I may pass out. Another climax of my life, and again I freeze. I stand there, truly dumbfounded for the first time. I can't talk or think so I just stand there, rooted by some unknown force that has rendered me speechless. She smiles at me, her sweet, beautiful lips, so red and delicious. I want to kiss her back, but I feel myself slipping away instead. I need to leave. I need to process her declaration.

Did that just happen? I've been told before that I'm loved, but this seems so raw and real. I think I'm ready for it, this unknown type of intense love, so why am I walking in the other direction? Why am I headed through security and getting on this flight? I turn to see if I can find her before I board the plane, but she's already gone. I barely find my seat and sink into it hard. I shrink into a little ball and stare out window, my forehead pressed against the cold glass. I don't see anything. I barely even feel the cold.

In movies and in books, when the hero confesses love, she's met with joy and happiness and tears. When my hero announces her love for me, I run. Part of me is smacking myself in the head for being a complete jackass, while the other part is telling me to take my time and process the information. Am I ready to open myself up so completely with Ali? Can I give one hundred percent and love her the way she deserves to be loved? What happens if I do give her my heart and we build a life together, with her family, and she cheats on me? Can I handle another woman breaking my heart, all the while laughing at me as she and her new partner erase me? Again? I sigh.

I know I'm not being fair to Ali. I can't hold her responsible for what Crystal did to me, and I'm sure deep in my heart that she didn't cheat on me with Gennifer. This means that one of us will have to give up her life to be with the other. And it will be me because I can't tear Ali away from her family. I want them as much as she does.

Em, Robert, and Shakespeare are so angry with me right now. My poets are all about love and harmony, and they've been pushing me to open up to Ali since the moment we saw her. For months, we've been trying to evolve this relationship, and finally, finally she opens up to me and I clam up and run the other way. Shakespeare is beating his head against a wall, Robert is pacing, his hands clenched in tight fists in his pockets, and Emily is in the corner crying. I'm scared. I'm afraid to let myself go. Again. Thankfully, Mr. Frost shows compassion. He reminds me that in this world of uncertainties, we just want love. We want that irresistible desire to be irresistibly desired.

I know this, and the more we discuss, the larger an asshole I become. I realize that Ali is taking a risk by giving me her all. And she wants to. I have the perfect woman and I just left her hanging. I'm so upset with myself. I need off this plane. I need to see her and explain to her that I was overwhelmed by her confession, but I feel the same way. We both deserve the chance to be happy. Emily still isn't talking to me. I'm a bit worried.

By the time the plane lands, I'm completely exhausted, but I'm sure of certain things now. Ali truly loves me and I love her. I have for a long time now but never wanted to admit it for fear of rejection. Since we got back together, Ali has never given me a reason to doubt her faithfulness. She's available to talk, text, and email twenty-four seven. She has always been there for me. As we taxi toward our gate, I'm furiously typing on my phone, trying to find a flight back to Boston. There aren't any direct flights tonight, but realistically I know that I can't turn around. My meeting tomorrow can't be rescheduled, and the sooner I get it done, the sooner I can get back to Ali. I try calling her, but she doesn't answer.

"Ali, I'm going straight to your voice mail. Please call me when you get this."

I wait. I check my phone every few minutes while I'm waiting for my luggage, but still no Ali. Where the hell is she? I hope and pray she isn't completely pissed at me. I was a complete jerk. I break down and decide to call Avery.

She answers her phone after the fifth ring. "Hi, Avery. It's Beth. How are you?"

"Beth! I'm good. You missed me so much you had to call, huh?" she says.

"Of course! That's why I'm calling. To hear your voice," I say. "Actually, I'm trying to reach Ali and can't get her. Is she around?"

"Ah, you know, I'm not sure, really. She could be. She was here after she dropped you off, but then I think she left again." She couldn't be more vague if she tried. I stop myself from growling in frustration.

"Oh, okay. Well, if you see her, please have her call me. It doesn't matter what time. I'll be up for a bit."

"Sure. Well, I gotta go now. See you soon!" Avery hangs up and I realize that was a very strange conversation.

❖

I'm done unpacking and I'm in the kitchen baking. I still can't reach Ali and now I'm getting concerned. I hope she wasn't in an accident or somebody kidnapped her. God, I hate my imagination sometimes. I've checked my phone about a dozen times, but I don't have a single text or missed call. I throw myself back into my baking because I don't know what else to do.

I'm surprised when I hear a knock at the door. It's after ten p.m. It has to be somebody in the building because getting past Bruno and his loyal henchmen is virtually impossible. They always ring if we have visitors. That's why we pay the big bucks to live there. I look through the peephole and gasp. It's Ali! I unlock the door and fling myself at her. We hold each other tight, more so than usual. I finally peel myself away.

"Oh, my God! You're here! You're here! Are you okay?" I'm touching her everywhere to make sure she's okay and to make sure she really is here in front of me. I pull her inside and close the door.

"I didn't want you to leave me today," she says. I hold her. She feels so good in my arms. I lead her to the couch and we sit facing one another.

"I've been trying to reach you for hours." I can't believe I'm scolding her at a time like this.

"Beth, I realize I dropped a major bomb on you today and I'm sorry, but I just can't keep it in anymore. I know you need time to get settled back into a relationship, but I can't help the way I'm feeling." Ali gets up and starts pacing the living room. Obviously, she needs to talk.

Peace settles over me because I love her, too, but I want to tell her when she's ready. Or when she shuts up long enough for me to say it. "I'm sure you aren't ready for a serious commitment yet, but this sucks. I hate leaving you every few weeks. I hate it when you leave me every few weeks. I can't stand it. I know I'm spoiled and I get what I want, but I really want you in my life every day. Not just a week here and there." She sits back down facing me. "I love you and I want to make us work. I want to move in together, and if you want to stay in Chicago, I'll move here. I want you. I've never wanted anything more. Ever." She starts to cry.

That does it. I'm completely overwhelmed, and because she's crying, I start crying. I wipe away her tears and can't help but smile at her. This beautiful woman, my dream come true, is confessing her love for me. I have a thousand things to shout at once, but I need to calm down. I can't screw this up again.

"Hey, hey, Ali. Listen to me. Listen to me," I say. There's so much vulnerability in her eyes that I'm suddenly filled with an incredible desire to protect her, take care of her, and love her forever. "I don't know why you think it's too soon for me to feel love or want this as much as you do, okay?" I run my hands through her long hair, tucking it behind her ears. "Yes, I've had it rough and yes, you're my first real relationship after Crystal, but I couldn't be happier. You're everything to me, and I've never loved anyone more than I love you."

She looks at me with such hope.

"I hate this separation, too. I don't care about Chicago. I only moved here because this is where my work is. I can live anywhere. I want to be with you. I know it's fast, but when you know something's right, then you should dive in. I hate all of this time we waste apart," I say. "I can sell this place tonight with one phone call."

"Are you serious?" Ali grabs my hands and pulls me to her.

"About which part?" I laugh. "I kind of said a lot in a short amount of time."

"About everything."

"I wouldn't have said it if I wasn't one hundred percent certain. I didn't want to say anything to you because you're Ali Hart, incredible musician. You, who you are, your fantastic family. It's unbelievable. I'm the luckiest girl in the world."

I'm smiling, because I'm a hot, sappy mess. Ali presses into me, kissing me with a mixture of pure joy and deep passion. I lean back, bringing her with me so that we're horizontal. She's frantically trying to rip off my clothes. The shrill of the timer on the oven stops us.

"Hang on." I slip out and head to the kitchen. Ali sits up and watches me. I can feel her gaze the entire time. I'm not nervous anymore. I pull the cookies out and leave them on the stovetop to cool. I steal a quick look at Ali. She's gazing at me with unabashed love, nothing hidden or guarded like before.

"I love you," I say, simply and quietly. I walk over to her and hold out my hand. "Let's go to bed and then we'll figure all of this out." Ali smiles her wicked grin at me and reaches out. We both gasp at the jolt that races through us as our hands touch and fingers entwine.

About the Author

Kris Bryant grew up a military brat, living in several different countries before her family settled down in the Midwest when she was twelve. Books were her only form of entertainment overseas, and she read anything and everything within her reach. Reading eventually turned into writing when she decided she didn't like the way some of the novels ended and wanted to give the characters she fell in love with the ending she thought they so deserved. Earning a B.A. in English from the University of Missouri, Kris focused more on poetry, and after some encouragement from her girlfriend, decided to tackle her own book. Jolt is her first novel. In her spare time, Kris enjoys traveling, hiking, photography, spending time with her Westie pup, Molly, and hanging out with her family.

Books Available From Bold Strokes Books

Rest Home Runaways by Clifford Henderson. Baby boomer Morgan Ronzio's troubled marriage is the least of her worries when she gets the call that her addled, eighty-six-year-old, half-blind dad has escaped the rest home. (978-1-62639-169-7)

Charm City by Mason Dixon. Raq Overstreet's loyalty to her drug kingpin boss is put to the test when she begins to fall for Bathsheba Morris, the undercover cop assigned to bring him down. (978-1-62639-198-7)

Edge of Awareness by C.A. Popovich. When Marija, a woman in the middle of her third divorce, meets Dana, an out lesbian, awareness of her feelings bring up reservations about the teachings of her church. (978-1-62639-188-8)

Taken by Storm by Kim Baldwin. Lives depend on two women when a train derails high in the remote Alps, but an unforgiving mountain, avalanches, crevasses, and other perils stand between them and safety. (978-1-62639-189-5)

The Common Thread by Jaime Maddox. Dr. Nicole Coussart's life is falling apart, but fortunately, DEA Attorney Rae Rhodes is there to pick up the pieces and help Nic put them back together. (978-1-62639-190-1)

Jolt by Kris Bryant. Mystery writer Bethany Lange wasn't prepared for the twisting emotions that left her breathless the moment she laid eyes on folk singer sensation Ali Hart. (978-1-62639-191-8)

Searching For Forever by Emily Smith. Dr. Natalie Jenner's life has always been about saving others, until young paramedic Charlie Thompson comes along and shows her maybe she's the one who needs saving. (978-1-62639-186-4)

Blue Water Dreams by Dena Hankins. Lania Marchiol keeps her wary sailor's gaze trained on the horizon until Oly Rassmussen, a wickedly handsome trans man, sends her trusty compass spinning off course. (978-1-62639-192-5)

Let the Lover Be by Sheree Greer. Kiana Lewis, a functional alcoholic on the verge of destruction, finally faces the demons of her past while finding love and earning redemption in New Orleans. (978-1-62639-077-5)

Blindsided by Karis Walsh. Blindsided by love, guide dog trainer Lenae McIntyre and media personality Cara Bradley learn to trust what they see with their hearts. (978-1-62639-078-2)

About Face by VK Powell. Forensic artist Macy Sheridan and Detective Leigh Monroe work on a case that has troubled them both for years, but they're hampered by the past and their unlikely yet undeniable attraction. (978-1-62639-079-9)

Blackstone by Shea Godfrey. For Darry and Jessa, the chance at a life of freedom is stolen by the arrival of war and an ancient prophecy that just might destroy their love. (978-1-62639-080-5)

Out of This World by Maggie Morton. Iris decided to cross an ocean to get over her ex. But instead, she ends up traveling much farther, all the way to another world. Once she's there, only a mysterious, sexy, and magical woman can help her return home. (978-1-62639-083-6)

Kiss The Girl by Melissa Brayden. Sleeping with the enemy has never been so complicated. Brooklyn Campbell and Jessica Lennox face off in love and advertising in fast-paced New York City. (978-1-62639-071-3)

Vermilion Justice by Sheri Lewis Wohl. What's a vampire to do when Dracula is no longer just a character in a novel? (978-1-62639-067-6)

Taking Fire: A First Responders Novel by Radclyffe. Hunted by extremists and under siege by nature's most virulent weapons, Navy medic Max de Milles and Red Cross worker Rachel Winslow join forces to survive and discover something far more lasting. (978-1-62639-072-0)

First Tango in Paris by Shelley Thrasher. When French law student Eva Laroche meets American call girl Brigitte Green in 1970s Paris, they have no idea how their pasts and futures will intersect. (978-1-62639-073-7)

The War Within by Yolanda Wallace. Army nurse Meredith Moser went to Vietnam in 1967 looking to help those in need; she didn't expect to meet the love of her life along the way. (978-1-62639-074-4)

Desire at Dawn by Fiona Zedde. For Kylie, love had always come armed with sharp teeth and claws. But with the human, Olivia, she bares her vampire heart for the very first time, sharing passion, lust, and a tenderness she'd never dared dreamed of before. (978-1-62639-064-5)

Visions by Larkin Rose. Sometimes the mysteries of love reveal themselves when you least expect it. Other times they hide behind a black satin mask. Can Paige unveil her masked stranger this time? (978-1-62639-065-2)

All In by Nell Stark. Internet poker champion Annie Navarro loses everything when the Feds shut down online gambling, and she turns to experienced casino host Vesper Blake for advice—but can Nova convince Vesper to take a gamble on romance? (978-1-62639-066-9)

Switchblade by Carsen Taite. Lines were meant to be crossed. Third in the Luca Bennett Bounty Hunter Series. (978-1-62639-058-4)

Nightingale by Andrea Bramhall. Culture, faith, and duty conspire to tear two young lovers apart, yet fate seems to have different plans for them both. (978-1-62639-059-1)

No Boundaries by Donna K. Ford. A chance meeting and a nightmare from the past threaten more than Andi Massey's solitude as she and Gwen Palmer struggle to understand the complexity of love without boundaries. (978-1-62639-060-7)

Timeless by Rachel Spangler. When Stevie Geller returns to her hometown, will she do things differently the second time around or will she be in such a hurry to leave her past that she misses out on a better future? (978-1-62639-050-8)

Second to None by L.T. Marie. Can a physical therapist and a custom motorcycle designer conquer their pasts and build a future with one another? (978-1-62639-051-5)

A Kingdom Lost by Barbara Ann Wright. Without knowing each other's fates, Princess Katya and her consort Starbride seek to reclaim their kingdom from the magic-wielding madman who seized the throne and is murdering their people. (978-1-62639-053-9)

Season of the Wolf by Robin Summers. Two women running from their pasts are thrust together by an unimaginable evil. Can they overcome the horrors that haunt them in time to save each other? (978-1-62639-043-0)

The Heat of Angels by Lisa Girolami. Fires burn in more than one place in Los Angeles. (978-1-62639-042-3)

Desperate Measures by P. J. Trebelhorn. Homicide detective Kay Griffith and contractor Brenda Jansen meet amidst turmoil neither of them is aware of until murder suspect Tommy Rayne makes his move to exact revenge on Kay. (978-1-62639-044-7)

The Magic Hunt by L.L. Raand. With her Pack being hunted by human extremists and beset by enemies masquerading as friends, can Sylvan protect them and her mate, or will she succumb to the feral rage that threatens to turn her rogue, destroying them all? A Midnight Hunters novel. (978-1-62639-045-4)

Seneca Falls by Jesse Thoma. Together, two women discover love truly can conquer all evil. (978-1-62639-052-2)

Wingspan by Karis Walsh. Wildlife biologist Bailey Chase is content to live at the wild bird sanctuary she has created on Washington's Olympic Peninsula until she is lured beyond the safety of isolation by architect Kendall Pearson. (978-1-60282-983-1)

Night Bound by Winter Pennington. Kass struggles to keep her head, her heart, and her relationships in order. She's still having a difficult time accepting being an Alpha female—but her wolf is certain of what she wants and she's intent on securing her power. (978-1-60282-984-8)

Windigo Thrall by Cate Culpepper. Six women trapped in a mountain cabin by a blizzard, stalked by an ancient cannibal demon bent on stealing their sanity—and their lives. (978-1-60282-950-3)

The Blush Factor by Gun Brooke. Ice-cold business tycoon Eleanor Ashcroft only cares about the three Ps—Power, Profit, and Prosperity—until young Addison Garr makes her doubt both that and the state of her frostbitten heart. (978-1-60282-985-5)

Smoke and Fire by Julie Cannon. Oil and water, passion and desire, a combustible combination. Can two women fight the fire that draws them together and threatens to keep them apart? (978-1-60282-977-0)

Slash and Burn by Valerie Bronwen. The murder of a roundly despised author at an LGBT writers' conference in New Orleans turns Winter Lovelace's relaxing weekend hobnobbing with her peers into a nightmare of suspense—especially when her ex turns up. (978-1-60282-986-2)

Rush by Carsen Taite. Murder, secrets, and romance combine to create the ultimate rush. (978-1-60282-966-4)

The Quickening: A Sisters of Spirits novel by Yvonne Heidt. Ghosts, visions, and demons are all in a day's work for Tiffany. But when Kat asks for help on a serial killer case, life takes on another dimension altogether. (978-1-60282-975-6)

Love and Devotion by Jove Belle. KC Hall trips her way through life, stumbling into an affair with a married bombshell twice her age. Thankfully, her best friend, Emma Reynolds, is there to show her the true meaning of Love and Devotion. (978-1-60282-965-7)

The Shoal of Time by J.M. Redmann. It sounded too easy. Micky Knight is reluctant to take the case because the easy ones often turn into the hard ones, and the hard ones turn into the dangerous ones. In this one, easy turns hard without warning. (978-1-60282-967-1)

In Between by Jane Hoppen. At the age of 14, Sophie Schmidt discovers that she was born an intersexual baby and sets off on a journey to find her place in a world that denies her true existence. (978-1-60282-968-8)

Under Her Spell by Maggie Morton. The magic of love brought Terra and Athene together, but now a magical quest stands between them— a quest for Athene's hand in marriage. Will their passion keep them together, or will stronger magic tear them apart? (978-1-60282-973-2)